CASSIDY'S WAR

To my amazing husband, your steadfast faith in me has been the pillar of my confidence, always there to elevate me when my doubts would arise.

To my delightful children, you've been a fountain of inspiration. Your support has fueled my resolve to instill in you the same pride I hold for you both.

To my cherished friends and family, your unwavering support has been invaluable on this remarkable journey.

TRIGGER WARNING

This book includes explicit and graphic sexual content, featuring LGBTQ relationships and multiple partners. It also contains scenes of violence and death, and some characters may express views such as homophobia which readers may find offensive. While these are not the view of the author they are critical to the context of the story.

Please proceed with caution and prioritize your mental well-being. If you find these topics are distressing, you may want to skip this content or ensure you have support available.

"Thy sweet love remembered such wealth brings,
That then I scorn to change my state with kings."
William Shakespeare - Sonnet 29

Mount Hejha
Xeyoria
Verancas
Berjorus
Dreik
Halen
Lythenyal
Vrek
Sleavalon
Trikara
Eyre
Svaalgard
Vrejtundra
Quebbaterra
Iyt
Chundra
Zeiynte
Pyr
Vaar
Omimor
Kryd
Krogary
Trukeoyka
Dysianthor
Islands
Evrodrivia
Vruj

Cassidy's War unfolds in the fantastical world of Xeyiera, primarily within Eyre, the largest kingdom. Given the many references to various kingdoms, I have created the accompanying map to illustrate the geographical locations of each realm; from the rugged mountain ranges and serene beaches, to the barren deserts and lush swamps of Xeyiera.

Prologue

Cassidy

If I shut my eyes, perhaps I could pretend that this was a terrible dream. Echoing cries of the wounded would be absent. Oppressive silence of the deceased would not deafen me. These desolate wastelands, once my home, would not be mounds of ash. At least Estoria, the capital of Eyre, would still be standing.

The distinctive metallic aroma of blood filled my nostrils. My teeth rattled from the clatter of metal swords. The sickening ripping of flesh made my stomach turn. This War caused a division in our Kingdom, each side made up of our own people. Innocent citizens of Estoria were fighting against their friends, neighbors, and even members of their own family.

People of Estoria have always been fiercely loyal to the crown, willing to sacrifice their life and freedom for the King they serve. The passing of the former King meant they had to choose who out of sons, Logan and Jax, they trusted enough to rule their precious kingdom of Eyre. I regret attending the Masquerade of Whispers. I would not have met either one of the Princes and suffered at the hands of Fate, nor fall victim to the stupidity of love.

Estoria would still be intact, not amid the chaos of this raging war resulting with its buildings now nothing more than rubble and dust. Blazing infernos swept across the city surrounding the battleground where my two loves are battling fiercely to win my hand in marriage; Both desiring to become my only surviving soulmate.

Whoever wins, I will lose. The war will end with only one outcome.

ONE

Cassidy

The eagerly expected letter arrived this morning with a royal seal. It was addressed to Father, Mr. William Ryvera. With trembling hands, I took it to him. The corners of the letter flapped like a caged bird trying to flee. I knew what this letter contained before he opened it; my heart sank, knowing what Father's reaction would be. He pried it from my vice-like grip, staring at the seal. The smirk on his face revealed that he also anticipated the arrival of this letter.

A diligent man, Father had tried to provide us with a stable life. Although we were far from rich, we were comfortable, well fed and did not have the financial struggles that many others suffered in this part of Estoria. Father's face showed the hardships of life and his continued efforts to keep it that way. This letter, though, could contain the very ticket to his early retirement.

The recently deceased King needed a successor, and soon. Traditionally, the throne would pass to his eldest son, but the King had decreed before his death that whichever of his two sons first fell in love and married would inherit the crown.

City folk whispered about it for the past week. Now this letter in my hand, could confirm their theory. It seemed surreal. For centuries, the royal family married beyond Eyre, introducing new bloodlines from unfamiliar kingdoms. These people would grace us with their presence and gift the King with the most beautiful offspring.

These children and their entire existence were shrouded in mystery. The tradition to keep their identities hidden had come as a result of a planned assassination many decades ago. Ever since this attack on King Rufus III, the public only caught a brief glimpse of the royal children during celebrations such as a wedding or coronation of the next monarch, returning to faceless phantoms afterward. I imagined their life was miserable and lonely, being trapped in isolation from society and plagued with paranoia.

For once the gossip had been correct. I watched from the window with bated breath as messengers delivered hundreds of invitations to fathers of eligible women between the ages of eighteen and twenty-two. My eighteenth birthday passed last month. I was now one of them.

Father's eyes flicked up to mine as soon as the seal brushed against his fingertips. His glare silently judged my reaction. If my face reflected the inner turmoil that whirred through my head, he would have known how I felt about it. I had dreaded coming of age, and I hated the responsibilities and expectations that came with adulthood. I had seen how they burdened my parents - forcing them to choose what they believed to be morally correct or follow the demands of the Elders.

When I said nothing, he sighed and ripped it open without further haste. "The Royal Princes Logan and Jax Silverthorne would like to proffer this formal invitation to request the eldest daughter of the Ryvera family to attend the Masquerade of Whispers on Saturday the 28th of May. It is with their greatest insistence that Cassidy attends. The two Royal Princes wish to impose that all invitees dress suitably for this formal occasion, including the use of a full or partial mask. Failure to comply will cause the invite to be rescinded."

I imagined myself sporting the requested attire. I already felt beads of sweat forming on my brow and the embarrassment from looking like a jester. My heart pummeled in my chest and my stomach lurched while Father continued to silently read the contents of this letter. Soon I would be confronted with my worst fear, one that petrified me beyond reason; meeting my soulmate. If he found me, not only would it mark us as Mates, to whom my soul would be bound for the rest of my life, it would also mean the end of freedom.

Father's mouth curled into a smile, and his eyes sparkled in delight. "You, my girl, are going to the ball!" he chuckled as his arms forced me into a deathly tight embrace. "You will win the heart of a Prince. Mark my words!"

I let out a groan. Before receiving this letter, my parents had been content with my lack of ambition. I did not desire great wealth; being happy was my goal as I pursued the humble career of a healer. I did not desire, nor was I prepared, for lifelong commitments with anyone. The sanctimonious ritual was a sacred bond, joining two souls together until the mercy of death took one from the other.

Traveling to kingdoms beyond Eyre had been my dream since I was a little girl. The very edges of the Xeyiera were calling my name, begging to be explored. Nothing would stop me once I stepped foot out of Estoria's barricaded walls, eager to start that adventure. Most of its inhabitants, like my parents, spent their entire lives imprisoned in this city, but I did not want to be one of them.

I knew Estonia had anything we could ever want, and a few opportunities were available to fulfill my wish allowing me to travel across the world of Xeyiera. I was unable to land a punch which eliminated my chance of becoming a warrior. Lacking the gift of gab, the life of a trader was not for me. Thankfully, my ability to heal would allow me to get out of Estoria and Eyre for good.

The Elders all had special abilities: telepathy, telekinesis, and healing, to name a few. In Eyre, it was uncommon for people to inherit abilities, the Elders only gifted them to citizens to carry out specific roles and duties in the Kingdom.

As far as I was aware, other than the connection forged when two soulmates consummated their bond. Telepathy was not a gift readily issued to citizens; how I came to have this connection with Flynn was a complete mystery.

It was rare that humans possessed the healing ability. Many healers were summoned to serve in hospitals around Eyre. Between my sister and me, only I had inherited this 'gift' from Mother. We were similar, not only by our ability to heal but also in looks. She wanted me to follow in her footsteps and hoped that one day I would replace her as the Leading Midwife of Estoria; the crème de la crème of midwives.

Few people with healing abilities were chosen because of the midwifery's complex and delicate nature. To perform such a role, one had to be among the very best healers. Although it brought honor and the utmost respect, it also meant she could never leave the city. Her expertise and abilities required constant availability. Day or night, she would see patients whenever help was needed. That life was not my desired future. Time was running out, and I was yet to establish my career in healing within the military division. Although the thought of war and conflict petrified me, that was the only field that would guarantee a life filled traveling throughout Xeyiera.

Father's eyes gleamed with expectation, hinting at his serious consideration of the idea of me becoming a future Queen. Recognizing his frustration, I sighed and told him, "Papa... I can't go." I watched as his face contorted with rage, his skin a deep shade of crimson as the vein in the side of his head bulged.

He crumpled the letter into a ball, throwing it to the floor in anger. He yelled at Mother to talk some sense into me. "Sienna, I had the impression that our daughter was an intelligent girl." His eyes lingered on me for a moment before he stormed out of the room.

Guilt flooded me as I was unable to fulfill Father's wish. By refusing his command and disobeying his orders, I would bring shame to the family. If only I could suppress the need to be free. If I attended the masquerade, I may be paired with one of them. Having a royal Prince was a fantasy shared by all girls across Estoria - except for me. It did not matter if I was not the prettiest woman. I was fond of my plain, average appearance. It was a blessing to have a face that was hard to extinguish within a crowd, allowing me to pander through life unnoticed. Fate did not care about appearances. It mattered not if I was a gruesome witch. My mate would always be attracted to me.

Melody rushed to my side, unable to contain her buzz of excitement, and shrieked, "I'm so jealous!" Entranced by her fantasies, she cooed about the attractiveness of both Princes. Having not seen them before, everyone was unsure of what to expect. There was a possibility that they looked like trolls.

Mother pouted, showing her disappointment. "Why must you act like a petulant child?" Like a knife, her voice sliced through the air, which created a stark contrast to its typically floaty and melodic tones. I recoiled, not accustomed to the coldness that now emanated from her. My mother had always been supportive and empathetic but now as her hand rested on my shoulder, I felt the cold and abrupt shift in her demeanor. "Cassidy, there are no excuses. You must go."

Mother frowned as she tried to flatten the invitation that was now a ball of parchment paper. Her eyes scanned the letter. "Cassidy, you were specifically requested. To ensure that our family is not dishonored, you *will* attend. End of discussion."

With stubbornness, I crossed my arms. Though it did not matter if I wanted to attend, I needed to make it clear to both parents that I was not happy.

It had been ingrained in all Estorian children that any form of disrespect or disobedience would be punished. If directed toward the royal family, it would even be considered treason, for which death was the punishment. In this case, punishment was likely for those who refused a royal invitation.

The importance of this event resonated in the room; the silence was palpable. Since the former king removed the traditional linear succession of the throne, the kingdom had fallen into unrest. The people needed structure and guidance from a leader *soon*. If this Masquerade Ball was unsuccessful, the kingdom would be under the sole rule of the Elders once more. *No one wants that.*

I nodded my head, reluctantly accepting my fate as tears stung my eyes. A lump formed in the back of my throat. The walls felt like they were closing in on me, suffocating me as they constricted my lungs like a vice. I struggled to speak. *I do not want to go. I do not want to play along in this game of theirs,* but I knew I had no choice in the matter. Reluctantly, I mumbled "Okay," avoiding eye contact with Mother.

Melody gave me a sympathetic look; her expression made her appear much older than fourteen years. "It would be great if both you and Flynn were honest about dating each other. Both of you should just get it over with and make it official!" She huffed, rolling her eyes in annoyance. Mother shuddered as her eyes narrowed at Melody. Her silent glare insisted on my sister's silence.

A small smile teased the corners of my mouth. An automatic reaction to the sass my sister exuded. Flynn, my oldest and dearest friend, was like a brother to me. There had never been any romantic feelings between us. We were inseparable, and people thought we were to be mates. It did not matter how many times we protested our friendship, Melody, along with everyone else, was convinced Flynn and I were more than friends. *If only she knew the truth...*

I slumped onto my bed and stared at the ceiling. My mind envisioned the places I so desperately wanted to explore, from the luscious, green mystical forests to the dusty, dry lands of the desert. I yearned to feel the sand between my toes as I gazed across the horizon, and faced the edge of the world, although it seemed to lie beyond my grasp. I wished that it could have been as simple as being mated with Flynn, a calm and gentle soul whose genuine kindness warmed my heart. He would never have held me back, or joined me. He had something in Estoria that compelled him to stay; a quest to find his father.

No one knew Flynn's father apart from his mother, who sadly passed away last year. Growing up without a father was rare in Estoria. For years Flynn had pestered his mother, even as she lay dying, hoping to be reunited with him, but his attempts were in vain. It appeared the identity of his father had been taken to her grave. She had left behind very little clues to aid him. I thought only those destined could communicate telepathically: two souls joined as one could think as one. Although Flynn and I knew we were not mates, we were still able to communicate telepathically ever since we were children.

Almost as if summoned, Flynn's voice sliced through my thoughts, *Cassidy, is it true? Did you get an invitation?"*

"Unfortunately, so," I responded without moving my lips.

"I got an invite too," he whispered. *"As did my brothers; Mason and Rik."* My brows furrowed at his revelation. *"I know why they are inviting us. I think the city is trying to play matchmaker, not just for the two Royal Princes, but for everyone."* Flynn pressed on.

I stared into space, my brain still trying to process the news. Flynn sighed, *"They seem intent for us Estorians to marry among ourselves. To repopulate the capital. Also, I fear it's a means to weasel out those who don't love correctly."*

Each passing day served as a stark reminder of the city's upcoming event. Days before, the city was adorned with new decorations for the Masquerade. Shops bustled with people as they purchased ball gowns, suits, and masks. Each day that passed, the city walls closed in around me a little more.

"They seem to want us Estorians to marry among ourselves." Flynn's words played in my head in a continuous loop, instilling a fear that I had never known.

The thrum of the city surrounded us as we traipsed along, our hands laden with shopping bags. We had gone looking for garments neither of us particularly wanted to wear. Our reluctance to attend the Masquerade of Whispers may have been shared between us, but the rest of Ralco buzzed with excitement.

"Don't panic," he soothed, startling me out of my reverie, as his arm draped around my shoulders. "You're not the one with something to hide," he added through gritted teeth. His voice was comparably different from his usual melodic tones. Fear seeped into his eyes and oozed from his pores.

I tried to steady my voice, to hide the uncertainty behind my words. "They won't find out, Flynn," I told him. "Though I don't understand why they see being in love with the same sex as wrong."

Clause 4a in the Rules of Conduct clearly stated that same-sex relationships were forbidden, even if Fate had paired them. No one knew why. It was believed that the Elders were so fixated on the growth of the population that they were willing to overrule Fate to ensure the continuation and growth of Eyre. There were many clauses that idolized heterosexual behavior and repressed all other forms of sexuality, but Clause 4a was the most feared. It sentenced those found to be gay, male or female, to death. His arm tightened around me as he steered me into a small side alley, away from prying eyes.

There was a reluctance in his eyes that showed his unwillingness to voice his words aloud. *"I need you to make me a promise,"* he said silently, allowing his mind to open the link to mine. *"It is a big ask, and I'm not sure if I have any right to ask you..."*

"I'll do it, Flynn." I interrupted. *"If it prevents your secret from being revealed, I will do it."* I had read his thoughts. He needed me to make him my 'chosen' mate, to consummate with him, so to shield his true sexuality. An act that was not unpopular but not was not favored by the Elders.

We stood in silence, our inner voices frantically speaking; yet to the untrained eye, we were simply staring at each other. We devised a plan. My heart pounded. The weight of the task he asked crushed me, squeezing the air from my lungs and forming a pit in my stomach. I should refuse to bind myself to him, to make him my 'chosen' mate, knowing he would never be able to love me like a mate should. I would suffer a lifetime of unfulfillment with the absence of *real love*. Yet if I did not agree not only would my life-long friendship with Flynn crumble before my very eyes, but should he be executed; his death would forever stain my conscience. His secret will burden both of us, risking dishonor against the Elders and their Rules of Conduct. It will not end well for either of us, should the truth be exposed. Accepting his request had sealed my Fate should the Elders ever know

I recalled the day Flynn shared his darkest secret with me all those moons ago. He admitted the guilt of his homosexuality that he entrusted me with. It was a secret so vast that could only be shared with one person. As Flynn told me, he appeared slightly relieved, as if a weight had been lifted. I watched his face cloud over, as he stood before me, appalled at himself for something he could not control. It was clear how heavy and oppressive his secret truly was.

When our eyes met again, Flynn's pain stabbed at me like a sword to the heart. "I'm sorry I have to ask this of you," he whispered, his hand tucking a loose curl behind my ear. "I wish I could love you as you deserve to be loved...."

"Flynn, your secret will die with me. I promise," I told him, my hand in his. "You will make an excellent mate, even if it is *unconventional*." I tried my hardest to smile, but his sorrow was suffocating us both.

"Look, at least you know all my terrible and irritating habits!" I made an attempt to lighten the gloomy tension that had fallen over us. "Plus, I already know that you snore!" I added, nudging him playfully in the ribs with my elbow.

"You are something special, Cassidy," he sighed, as he combed his hair with his fingertips.

We snaked our way back into the crowded street, suddenly engulfed in the chaos once more as we began our journey to our corners of the city. His hand was still in mine. "Any guy would be lucky to have you as a mate, a real one..." he glanced at me quickly, before tightening his grip. "I'm sorry if I prevent you from having that future, that mate, you deserve."

Estoria was split into five boroughs: Fic, Faelfoy, Thamsleep and Winro were the boroughs that divided the square city into quarters, whereas Ralco was the one that sat in the center of them all. It was the central hub where the castle stood.

We walked to the southeastern quarter of Ralco; the streets grew darker and dirtier, our borough, Fic, sat on the other side. Renowned for its industrial heritage, large factories produced the items sold in the shops inside Ralco, and they were also traded to foreign lands where I had wished to travel.

Only the residents of Fic frequented its streets did not get the same treatment as the boroughs that welcomed visitors such as Faelfoy and Winro. These two districts lined either side of Estoria's fortified entrance. Full of taverns and hotels, they housed the majority of the travelers to Estoria.

I wanted to be among them, to hear of their stories and their experiences from lands afar, but those boroughs were home to only the elite members of society; the richest of us all. It seemed the city clean-up was reserved for those three boroughs only to uphold the rich and thriving reputation Estoria held across the kingdom of Eyre and throughout Xeyiera.

In theory, Faelfoy should have been our home borough, along with the other families of midwives. Mother's right as Estoria's lead midwife, was to live in The Matron's Quarters. A segregated community designed for the families of midwives looking after each other's young while the women carried out their midwifery duties for the city.

However, as Father owned the city's only blacksmith and artillery factory, we were housed in a shabby and cluttered part of Fic, where houses stood too close together, crammed like sardines. The inhabitants were hard-working and colorful characters who drank too much and swore like sailors. When I was younger, I found them entertaining, yet now I found them intimidating and lecherous.

Perhaps if I had lived in Faelfoy, I would not have been so desperate to travel beyond Estoria's immeasurably high stoned walls that seemed to tower over us all. Initially constructed after the last war many decades ago to prevent Estoria from attacks. Now their sole purpose was to keep its residents imprisoned.

The invading armies of Sladebaun decimated our population many moons ago, taking many of our greatest warriors. I wondered if that was why the Elders wanted us to mate, in order to remain in Estoria. People were less likely to leave the city if they had a reason to stay.

"Catch you later," Flynn smiled, giving my hand one last squeeze before walking to the farthest end of the terraced houses. "See you tomorrow?" His brow knitted together as his eyes sought mine.

Without returning his look I nodded. Out the corner of my eye I spotted the distinctive look of disapproval on Father's face as he peered out the window. *Shit, he does not look happy.*

"Cassidy, what do you think you are doing?" he bellowed as soon as my feet stepped over the threshold. "You cannot fraternize with the opposite sex so openly!" I bowed my head in apology. "You know it is frowned upon to be friends with a man now that you are of age." He cleared his throat as he stood ominously at the far end of the lounge. "Besides, the masquerade is in two days..."

"Sorry Papa..." I mumbled. "But it's not like I am fraternizing with an enemy! Our families have been friends since Mama helped birth him! We have been friends my entire life. I won't stop being his friend now that I am eighteen!" I felt my voice get louder then my temper flared, instantly recoiling as Father's face reddened in anger. "Papa... he is my *only* friend."

His face softened as he stepped closer to me. "I know, Pumpkin, but we must do things the proper way, the Estorian way. Even if we may not agree, it is simply the way things are. You are an adult now, Cassidy. It is time you started acting like one." I clamped my mouth shut as fresh tears sprung to my eyes.

I hated turning eighteen, and being an adult in such a regimented kingdom. The Rules of Conduct dictated our lives. I loathed their cultish indoctrination. From the moment Estoria's children set foot in the classroom, it was spooned into their mouths.

Their rights and wrongs were forged centuries ago and forced to be implemented into a very different, modern world that we live in today. I glanced at Father. I saw his irritation and anger.

"Well, Cassidy, I forbid you from seeing him again. Do you understand?" Father declared in a huff.

Melody gasped as she stood in the doorway. The vase of fresh-cut flowers she had in her hands plummeted to the floor, shattering upon impact, spraying fragments of glass and water droplets into the air, while the heads of the flowers detached from the stems and scattered across the tiled floor. "Papa... that's not fair," I tried to argue, my attempt weak and pathetic. He remained silent while his eyes flickered between my sister and me.

"Life isn't fair, girls, it's about time you learned that... and fast," Mother said as she appeared behind Melody, her eyes sweeping over the shattered vase. "It is beneficial for all when we acknowledge we follow the rules, not make them." She scowled, stepping over the debris, and stood beside Father. "Disobedience leads to serious consequences for those who flout rules or deceive the Elders. They are not as lenient as the King. Unless you want to incriminate your father and me, Cassidy, you will stay away from Flynn."

Mother's eyes narrowed as they locked onto mine. I felt the heaviness of her words like a slap in the face. It was as if she knew of the promise I had made to him. My promise to protect his secret. She shook her head slowly, her mouth pulled into a tight line. "Remember what happened to Pascale?"

I tried hard not to remember. The horrors of that night had tormented me with nightmares for weeks after. I nodded slowly, my eyes dropping to the floor. The Elders took a breach of Clause 4a seriously. However, Pascale served as a severe reminder not to breach Clause 3d: *Never interfere with another's mate.* As a testament to their intolerance for rule-breaking, the Elders served him no warning or trial. He was executed without being given a chance to justify his actions.

Mother bowed her head for a moment, her lips pursed in a taut line. When she looked up, her eyes were watery. I could tell she was trying to deny tears from falling.

"Good, so if you do not wish your father or me the same Fate, you will obey and follow the Rules of Conduct..." her voice hardened as she crossed her arms over her chest. "Without argument."

My legs could not carry me fast enough away from them, out of my house and beyond my street. Houses and factories became a blur in my peripheral vision as I ran, whizzing by as indistinguishable masses as I tried to clear the thoughts from my head. I remembered the images of Pascal's cold, lifeless eyes as his head rolled to a stop at my feet.

I had been eight when I unintentionally sent our neighbor, Pascale, to his death. My words were twisted to seem sinister, unbeknownst to me. I had condemned him lying, of acting against the wishes of the Elders, and against The Rules of Conduct. Pascale had merely kissed Mother on the cheek, a familiar term of endearment from a friend. The Elders were misconstrued, deeming the act as indecent, a breach of Clause 3d. Despite Pascale being twice as old as Mother, an old friend of my grandfather's, and a prominent figure within our entire family, the Elders still sentenced him to death.

There was no trial. One day they stormed into our home unannounced, and vehemently interrogated me with their confusing and repetitive questions until I wet myself in fear. The next thing I remembered is Pascale's head being cut clean from his neck, in the living room of our house, his headless body crumpling to the floor, his head rolling along like a stray football.

"Cassidy! What's the matter?!" His worried voice filtered through these thoughts. He had felt my pulse race and my body quiver in fear. I tried to push my trepidation aside, to shield him from the panic that drowned me. Yet I could do nothing to stop my body's natural reaction to the alarm and terror Pascale's death inflicted upon me.

"Flynn, I'm sorry..." I responded in my mind as I powered through the streets, heading to the one spot where I could guarantee absolute silence and isolation. This was the most beautiful spot in the whole of Estoria: The Forgotten Lake. That wasn't

its real name, it may not even have one, but that was how I referred to it. Ever since I discovered it by mistake when I was younger, taking a wrong turn on my way back from my father's blacksmiths, it held a special place in my heart. It almost instantly became my sanctuary to escape whenever I felt overwhelmed with emotions.

Everything there was free to thrive; flowers bloomed among the greenery, as wildlife grazed on the untouched fruits of the trees, all unthwarted by human interaction. All was how nature had intended it to be, not cultivated into the Elder's perception of what beauty *should* look like.

"I need some space," I added before shutting him out and blocking our connection. The sinking feeling crept into the pit of my stomach. The Elders would have a killing frenzy. All of us would have our heads on spikes at the entrance of Estoria if they knew the truth.

The lake was still, its surface smooth and reflective, like that of a mirror. Tall weeping willows hung over the banks and reached down to the water's edge. The only sounds that could be heard were the soft harmonious tunes of the birds nesting in their branches, and the irregular thumping of my heartbeat as it pounded in my ears.

As I neared the lake's edge, I glimpsed at my reflection in the water. Tousled in the wind, my crazy brown curls spiraled in all directions. It reminded me of Medusa's many snakes as they writhed upon her head with minds of their own. My green eyes were pools of algae compared to the clear water before me. Tears silently fell as I grieved for the traumas of my past, for the uncertainty of my future and for the loss of my friendship with Flynn.

In the furthest part of Fic, my little sanctuary existed. The Forgotten Lake sat just before the stonewall. This small haven was where nature grew freely, and wildlife thrived uninterrupted and unnoticed by the inhabitants of the industrial borough. Every time I came here, it was deserted, as if abandoned for nature. Vines wrapped around trees, and grass was knee high with long-stemmed wildflowers. It was the perfect place to sit and contemplate life's choices.

A honey bee flitted from one flower to another going about his monotonous routine of collecting pollen for its hive, completely unfazed as I stood at the lake's edge. The longer I stared on its shimmering surface, the more my reflection seemed to change. My eyes darkened, and my body crumpled and slouched. The heaviness of the potential consequences weighed me down.

There was a sudden snap behind me, followed by a rustle of leaves. I spun on my heel to face my pursuer.

Two

Ralco buzzed with insufferable energy, and I needed a respite from the meticulous planning and preparations that were being undertaken at the castle. I was unable to manage any more of this ridiculousness, this ludicrous spectacle that was to take place in the next few days. It made a mockery of the lineage, and it was a joke of the natural succession of the throne. As the eldest son of the King, it was natural that I would be his successor. After all, I had been training my whole life to deal with the pressure of such a task, unlike my younger brother, Jax, who coursed through life with everything offered on a silver platter. As he was the youngest heir, the least likely to be crowned King, *or so we all thought,* he enjoyed the privilege of having his every need attended to. He reaped the rewards of everyone else's hard work.

It had been several weeks now, but I was still furious when Father publicly announced from his deathbed that his successor would be the first one to marry and bond with a life partner - an almost impossible task given our limited freedom. None of the princesses from across Xeyiera had lived up to my expectations or held my interest beyond their initial beauty. An exotic bride never appealed to me.

"The Kingdom needs stability. The power of an alpha and the mercy of a woman," he had said to Jax and me. *"Do either of you care about fulfilling your responsibilities as the next King? One of you will be King when I am gone. That son must produce heirs to maintain our legacy. That can only happen when you choose your mate."*

Over the past year he became weaker and his internal organs failed him. Though he remained as intimidating and ferocious as he always had been upholding his duties as the monarch of Eyre, at the time I felt compelled to correct him; *in fact, we do not choose our mate, only when destiny intended would they find us.* Yet when I looked at him and saw his scowl, it seemed imperative to remain silent. Later that evening, he was dead.

It had been Jax's idea to host this masquerade ball, a way for us to mingle with women within our age range, hoping one of our mates would be there. It will be the first time in over twenty-three years that members of the public would be welcomed into the castle. Reluctantly, I had to admit that it was a rather clever idea to incorporate masks so that the tradition of revealing our face did not happen until the royal wedding. I was intrigued to learn about personality before judging physical appearance.

This had never been done. I had only observed the people of Estoria from a distance, forbidden to mingle with them. We had exhausted our options of available foreign princesses, those who remained were still children. It was only because of the Elders' threat to usurp our inheritance by appointing someone else to be king had my brother conjured such an idea.

As I reached the forest the bordered the edge of Fic, an alluring scent caught my attention and unseen hands dragged me through the thick brush of pine trees. Before me should have been the towering walls that surrounded Estoria yet instead a serene and forgotten lake stood before me. I was shocked, it had not been marked on any of the maps I had studied in the castle. But I was not the first person to discover this secret place. I was not alone, someone was already there. There was a woman whom I had never seen before, as still as a statue with her hair cascading down the back of her black lace dress that billowed in the wind, making her look ethereal in the soft glow of dusk. Like a goddess, she seemed to emit an aura around her, drawing me to her. As I took a step forward, a branch snapped under my foot. Silently cursing myself, I moved out of sight, hiding behind a shrub, but the leaves rustled which gave away my location.

"Who's there?" she called out. Her voice was a sweet melody, pulsating my eardrums. I wanted to hear from her again.

I waited with bated breath as I tried not to move a muscle.

"Stop being a coward and show yourself!" she shouted, drawing herself upright, appearing much taller and seeming confident despite the croak in her throat that hinted otherwise.

I stepped out of the shadows, no longer caring about the tradition of our shielded identity that was in place for my safety. For some unknown reason, I felt like I could trust her. I wanted to get closer to her and learn more about her; who she was, and why she was here. *Why was I being drawn to her?*

"Who are...you?" she asked, her voice catching in her throat as I approached her. I gravitated toward her until I was a few feet away, my curiosity and compulsion like that of a moth to a flame.

Her aura glowed brighter as I drew closer, emitting a warmth that washed over me. I stopped when I got too close, there was as little as a few centimeters between us.

Without thinking, the impulse to touch and kiss her took control. My lips found hers. Shock flashed in her eyes. As deep and as rich as the finest emeralds, I could not tear my eyes away from them as they pierced me with confusion. Slowly her body softened, and her lips fluttered against mine, allowing my hands to rest on her waist.

Time froze, and Xeyiera stood still. Everything that had surrounded us faded into nothingness. All that I could focus on was her dazzling green eyes. I felt her reluctance to pull away from me. It was only then that I saw her cheeks glisten with tears; *I hadn't made her cry, had I?*

"Who are you?" her harmonious voice sent shivers up my spine. Her breath tingled against my face. The scent of lavender and vanilla radiated from her skin. She smelled delicious, but I also detected another fragrance; her arousal.

My hands still lingered on her waist as I drew her body closer. I never knew I could feel so drawn to someone I barely knew. My member twitched as her thighs pressed against mine.

"I'll tell you my name, if you tell me yours first," I teased, my mouth inches from hers.

She bit her bottom lip in contemplation. Her eyes never left mine. "Cassidy," she replied, her breath hot against my lips.

Now it was my turn. *Should I be honest?* I asked myself, as I parted her lips with my tongue. This girl had to be my mate. *The urge to defy rules for her must hold significance, right?*

"Cassidy...pretty name..." I whispered, as my hands wandered, one hand snaking up into her hair, holding the base of her head keeping her face close to mine, and the other held firm on the small of her back, pressing her body into mine.

Her chest rose and fell heavier than before as my lips lightly kissed her neck. She took a sharp breath as my lips lingered over the most sensitive and vulnerable part of her neck. Her pulse quickened as her jugular, vibrating hypnotically beneath my touch.

She lacked a mate and had little experience, that was certain. I would be her first with everything. The thought sent a thrill down my spine to my shaft. "I believe you should call me...*mate.*"

Her body tensed, and her head shook from side to side. "No..." she gasped, trying to back away. "No, no, no..." her eyes darted frantically, looking everywhere except at me.

I let her go and watched as she took three small steps back. Instinctively, I matched those steps, looking like we were performing a dance.

"Cassidy..." I leaned on her as she backed into a tree. *"Don't deny our attraction,"* I said silently, as my voice reached into her mind. If she could hear it, then my instinctive impression of her being my mate had to be true.

Her eyes flickered wide. Then her fear and realization kicked in. *She heard it!* She tried to move, but my body had her pinned, my erect member pressing against her virgin heat. My hand pulled her leg upward to position her better. I was unable to control my desire for her. I wanted to mark her, and consummate this bond I had eagerly awaited. Her mouth crashed against mine despite her prior objection.

"What the fuck, Cassidy?" my head whipped around to a voice from behind us. A tall, slender man, with shaggy blonde hair and bright blue eyes stood. His mouth gaped open in surprise, and his eyes narrowed as he watched our bodies disentangle.

"You already have a mate?" I frowned; my voice was bitter. "I see how it is..."

I felt her eyes follow me as I left the lake. They burned on my back as I weaved through the trees, hoping she would lose sight of me. Humiliation bubbled beneath the surface of my skin. *I cannot look back or show any sign of weakness.* The further I moved away from her the more our connection pulled me back. It took every ounce of energy to put one foot in front of the other so the distance between us got wider. She was the one for me. *How could I be so wrong?*

THREE

Cassidy's pounding heart, labored breathing, and intense fear flooded my mind. I had sought her out like a bloodhound on a hunt, following her distress signals, and using our telepathic connection to navigate her exact location. I thought she had been in danger, not caught up in a passionate embrace.

My jaw dropped. The epitome of all womanly desires was before me. The man was tall, dark-haired, and very handsome. His black, tailored shirt emphasized his bulging biceps, broad shoulders, and muscular torso, and he was aroused. A tent was pitched at the crotch of his jeans. She was too, as she grinded herself against it.

I could not take my eyes off of them. Their chemistry held my curiosity, but I had to stop them. Selfishly, I needed her to remain unmated and unbound if she was to conceal my secret.

It was not Cassidy I was watching. It was him. His erection. Imagining being in his arms instead of hers caused a stir in my nether regions. *A lifetime of denying my true sexuality would not be easy.*

I swore at her, unable to hide the hurt in my voice as I tentatively stepped closer toward them. I thought Cassidy would have told me, or at least I would have known through our bond that she had met someone, her mate. Yet the more I pondered it, the more I felt guilty. A pit in my stomach tore itself open again. She concealed it, being a good friend, she did not want me to feel guilty.

Her mate's face whipped around to face mine, while his dark brown eyes smoldered under his intense glare. His jawline clenched in anger as her leg instantly dropped back to the floor and her hands fell away from his face. A mix of anger and embarrassment consumed me. *How stupid was I to confuse her arousal for impending danger? Do I actually lust for her mate, or are those her feelings that I am confusing as my own?*

Finding our mate only happened once-in-a-lifetime. Once we stumbled upon it, we had one opportunity to accept. We had one time to unite our souls.

While staring at them, I focused more on him than her. He appeared older, perhaps not from Estoria. Maybe he was a visitor from a neighboring Kingdom. *This could be Cassidy's chance for freedom, but at what cost?*

The masquerade would soon arrive. My deep, dark secret was punishable by death. I needed her, and I expected her to fulfill her promise to help me. She was the only person I trusted, the only one who knew the truth. I could not let her mate take her away from me. *Though I may not have a choice.*

"How did you know I was here?" she gasped. Her eyes followed her mate as his solid mass disappeared among the trees. I felt her body pining for him.

"I thought you were in trouble and distressed!" I told her, rushing over to her. I scuffed my foot in the long grass, as my hands shoved into my pockets to hide my erection.

I quickly averted my eyes away from her to the spot among the trees where he had disappeared. "So, who is he?"

She shrugged as her eyes wandered to the lake, lost in her thoughts, her cheeks aflame in embarrassment. "Cass, be honest, how long have you two..."

She held up her hand, silencing me. "I had never seen him or met him before," she whispered breathlessly.

Through our telepathic bond her determination distracted her thoughts from him, willing herself to remain focused on the stillness of the water's surface and not look for him. She also tried, with great difficulty, not to show her frustration at their abrupt ending. Without warning she shut me out.

"Do you know who he is?" she asked, eventually breaking the awkward silence that had smothered us for several long moments. Her face slowly looked up at me as her mind allowed our connection to open again once more.

My eyes flew open, my mouth agape. "Who is he? Is he one of the King's sons?" My mind was spinning. If he was, it would explain why neither of us had seen him before, but that was too personal for a first meeting. *Unless he is her soulmate?*

"I'm sorry, Cass," I sighed. "If I'd have known, I would not have…"

She threw herself to the ground, a sobbing heap at the edge of the lake, her body quaking.

I stood and watched her, unable to move. My guilt anchored me as it swelled within, slowly crushing my chest, and rendering my brain useless. Cassidy shook her head, in an attempt to stop the visions of his kiss as she felt my inquisitive presence invade her thoughts once more.

"I'm glad you did, Flynn. I don't want to stay here." She sniffed. "But… we can't be friends anymore… I am forbidden from seeing you."

Her words pierced me like a thousand swords as she continued to speak.

"It is not safe for us to be friends." Her back was to me, but I could see her fear ignite once more, as the image of Pascale's corpse flashed through her mind, while her conversation with her parents unfurled in the silence that befell us.

Instantly, I recalled witnessing Elianne's execution, the first woman I had ever seen killed by a firing squad. It had been made into a public spectacle; an example made from her crime, of loving another woman, to instill the fear of breaking the Rules of Conduct. It worked, her death haunted me, a constant reminder of my own demise should my true sexuality be revealed.

I was twelve when she was murdered. Out of fear, I had never acted on my impulsive desires, until I met *him:* Jace. It was a chance encounter upon visiting Cassidy one day at her father's blacksmiths several months ago. The moment our eyes locked, the connection clicked into place. His sandy hair was slicked with sweat, and those coal-burning eyes rendered me speechless. I knew from the age of seven, it was wrong to feel this way. I attempted to change, but with Jace's encouragement I had begun to accept the lack of control over my desire. Jace was the first to instigate our secret romance, pulling me into the dark shadows of the blacksmith's a few weeks later, where his mouth crushed against mine with a passion I had never known before. It was he who persuaded me to partake in the illicit acts that would eventually doom us both.

Even with soot smudged across his face, he was attractive, with his angelic features. Soon, I would sneak to meet him in the workshop after hours of stealing quick, frantic kisses. These quick escapades had been enough, but several months later our relationship had progressed as the risk of getting caught grew with each passing day.

With every illicit meeting we became more careless. One day we may love openly and freely, but now was not the time; Elianne's death was a testament to that.

The night grew upon us quickly as darkness blanketed the sky. Distant stars poked through beside the half-full moon. I knew we had to go home; curfew was fast approaching.

"Flynn, the party... the promise..." she sniffed. "I will still keep my promise to you."

We strolled back in silence. Our parting of separate ways grew tense. Cassidy placed all of her focus on trying not to think of the stranger at the lake, while I skulked at the prospect of losing the alibi that protected my secret. I struggled to sleep that night. My dreams were filled with death and morbidity. I knew the Elders would kill anyone they believed helped disguise my secret. After me, Jace would be among the first to be executed, and then Cassidy. Only three of us knew, yet the Elders would accuse others of being aware of the conspiracy.

I tried to imagine a life without Jace: depriving myself of our stolen kisses and the rushed encounters that strengthened our bond. If I did not have him, life did not feel worth living, but was this forbidden love worth the risk of multiple lives being tragically cut short? We had already become too intimate during our illicit meetings.

Have we already gone beyond the point of no return? Is it too late for us?

FOUR

I was in the heart of the castle. It had taken me forever to navigate through the labyrinth corridors that made up the lower floor. Eventually I found the great hall, where the Masquerade of Whispers was hosted. My hands trembled as I pushed open the large oak door, startled by the loud creak of protest that cried out from the old iron hinges.

His scent was the first thing I smelled as I entered the castle. It seemed to permeate every corridor. Over the floral notes of perfume and musty undertones of cologne, I could still detect the faint essence of him. I knew he had to be close. My obsession allowed my senses to pinpoint his fragrance above all others, the instinct to find him yanked at my heart. It transported my mind back to the lake. I remembered our closeness, and how his lips felt against my body. I shivered in excitement. He was here, somewhere in this castle. I needed to find him to explain that he had misunderstood the connection between Flynn and me, though I was not sure how I could explain without revealing Flynn's secret. Nor could I explain why I wanted to make him understand. I had not wanted a mate, until I met *him*. Whoever he was.

My eyes scoured the crowds, trying to find him amid the overwhelming silver and gold decor. Even the bouquets of roses as their centerpieces; each rose had been dipped into the liquid metals, droplets trickled down their petals and stems. Small flickering candles lit the hall in a cozy, orange glow.

I looked for him as I walked through the hall, trying to figure out who I wanted. My body longed for his presence, but my head battled with the fanciful idea of traveling the realm, exploring the many kingdoms that exceeded Eyre. Yet my body's desire for his touch made me question if I could truly leave. *What if he is the one?*

I strolled through the hall, my eyes wide open, taking in the tastefully selected decorations that adorned the walls and hung from the ceiling, giving a tactfully sophisticated energy that exuded the wealth of the royal family. I arrived at the exact time stated on the invitation. It appeared most of those invited had arrived early.

My skin prickled under their watchful and curious eyes as I approached the bar area. The weight of the scrutiny in these predatory eyes lay heavy on my chest, crushing it. I tried to take a few deep breaths to steady my anxiety, but each one felt like I was inhaling fire as they burned my throat and lungs. I wanted to go home, yet the compulsion to see him one more kept me here.

"Just breathe, Cass," Flynn said in his soothing mental voice, as he watched me from across the room. *"It's only a few hours."*

I nodded my head, blocking my thoughts from him. *A few hours at the party, but what comes after?* My bones ached at the thought of it. Like a caged bird, I needed space to spread my wings.

"Well, this is a snooze fest." An exasperated sigh came from the stranger sat beside me, wearing an ominous mask with a long-curved beak. Only his honey-gold eyes and the small arrogant smirk were visible.

I turned my head to look at him properly. He wasn't the guy who was at the lake.

"I'm Chad. Can I get you a drink?"

"I'll get that." A voice cut across him, as he pushed his way between us, his plain white, expressionless mask turning to face me. Dazzling blue orbs shone through the small eye slits.

"I'm Prince Jax," his voice purred. "And you are?" He picked up my hand from my lap and brought it up to his mask, lifting it away slightly so he could kiss the back of it, revealing a small sliver of his face; smooth and clean-shaven.

Butterflies in my stomach, fluttering uncontrollably. "Cassidy," I replied automatically, my gaze still transfixed on his eyes, my heart now pounding hard against my rib cage. "I am Cassidy Ryvera."

His head tilted to the side, as if pondering whether he recognized the name. "My father owns the only blacksmith and artillery factory in Estoria."

He slowly nodded his head. "Well Cassidy, it is a pleasure to meet you," he said, downing his drink and getting to his feet.

I felt a small pang of sadness flit inside me. I was torn between wanting to keep his attention and wanting to remain anonymous. There was one thing I knew; I could not wait until this night was over. Feeling uncomfortable in this tight-fitting dress, my face mask was irritating my eyes and making my nose feel sweaty.

"Stop playing with your mask," Flynn hissed in my mind.

My hands fell from my face, trying to busy them with taking small sips from my champagne flute.

"Cassidy, may I have this first dance with you?" He bowed, grasping my hand, while the orchestra played in the grand hall.

I nodded my head robotic-like, allowing him to take my hand and lead us to the center of the hall.

No one was dancing. We side-stepped slowly to the melodic rhythm, and he added a spin to draw me close to his body.,

I heard his heavy breath beneath the mask.

"Tell me more about yourself, Cassidy," he murmured in my ear, as he held his arms around my neck.

"What do you want to know?" I could not hide my obvious discomfort. I never knew what to say in these situations, unable to gauge what they wanted to hear, and trying not to sound like a simpleton.

"Do you have a boyfriend?" The question came without hesitation, as he spun me away from him, and pulled me back in before draping me across his arm, my curls tumbling to the floor.

He dragged me back up to my feet, and our faces met.

"Nope. What about you?" I asked, allowing him to hold my waist as we swayed on the spot.

His chuckle instantly lightened the energy between us. "No, I definitely do not." I pouted, as he drew my hips in closer so that his member rubbed against my inner thighs.

"You know that was not what I meant." I sighed, as my thoughts were slipping away from the conversation. I focused on his throbbing member.

His eyes darkened, and his stare grew more intense. "I'm just teasing...I do not have a girlfriend either," he purred. "I am not bound to anyone." His muffled words were hot against my ear. "Yet..." he added, his voice so low I barely heard him.

As the dance drew to a close, he spun me around so his chest pressed firmly against my back, and his arms wrapped around my waist. The distinctive poke of his member against my buttocks surprised me. My eyes snapped open, feeling embarrassed and awkward.

"Cassidy..." he moaned, low and throaty. "You are a very special woman." His breath swept down my neck, hot and urgent, making every hair stand on end. The music had already ended, yet he showed no intention of letting me go. I was pressed up against him, in front of a room full of people.

Flynn stirred, and my eyes flitted to where he last stood, though he was no longer alone. A blonde-haired, slender woman in a red full-length dress was openly flirting with him. I felt a pang of guilt at his awkwardness. His eyes followed my line of vision.

"Do you know either of them?" he asked, slowly turning me around to face them.

"Flynn is a *friend*- I mean, he is a neighbor." I quickly corrected myself, biting my lip, hoping he never caught my slip of the tongue.

"That is Demi talking to him. She is a nice girl but very high maintenance," he chuckled, as his fingertips slowly guided my head back to face him. "She's my sister... my twin sister." He chuckled. "But don't worry, twin telepathy is a myth." He winked, pulling me aside. "Please excuse me for a moment. I will be right back."

I nodded, unable to do anything other than watch him walk away from me.

"Was that?" Flynn's voice cut through my clouded and confused thoughts.

"Yes, Flynn... that was Prince Jax."

A low whistle escaped him, piercing my ears as Flynn studied one of the elusive princes; Jax Silverthorne.

Dressed in a white blazer, with matching trousers, a black shirt tucked in underneath, accompanied by his blank white mask, he was incredibly easy to spot in the crowd. Our eyes followed his every move as he flitted between groups of people, mingling with all of the guests, before he went over to the podium.

Suddenly, the room fell silent. A loud cough resonated as Jax took hold of the microphone. "Hello? Can you all hear me?" His assertive tone demanded attention. His aura was powerful.

He looked and sounded the part of the next King of Eyre.

"Thank you all for attending the Masquerade of Whispers tonight. May your evening be unforgettable." He propped up his mask to reveal only his clean-shaven, square jawline and his handsome and confident smile.

I stared at him, completely in awe. His head snapped toward me, and his eyes fixated on mine, as if I was the only person in the room. "Tonight marks the start of something magical. So, enjoy yourselves while the night is still young."

Applause erupted as he slid his mask back down to cover his face once more.

I glanced toward Flynn, but he was no longer there, nor was the girl in red. *"Flynn, where did you go?"* I asked, but my words were blocked, rebounding back to me in a solemn echo.

"Interested in touring the castle?" Jax asked, his arm sneaking around the small of my back. "It's been some time since the castle has been open to the public, and it's not every day that a Prince will personally take you on tour."

I downed the last of the champagne, hoping it would give me a little extra confidence. I nodded, giving him a small smile. My head was spinning. His presence made me forget about my life's ambition to travel, to be free from Estoria and Eyre.

With his arm looped around my waist, we left the hall while the orchestra continued to play and the sound of laughter and conversations petered out, the further into the courtyard we walked. Large topiary trees, sculpted into various shapes, lined the flagstone path, which divided it into quarters. Neatly tended flower beds hugged lawns, as large lanterns softly lit our way in the darkness.

It was a beautiful, serene evening almost mirroring the stillness of the lake. My eyes flitted to the shadows that lurked in each corner, expecting to see the stranger from the lake.

I glanced at the castle's windows, wondering if he was inside. I did not realize Jax had stopped in the courtyard. Crashing into his chest was like walking straight into a brick wall. His muscular rib cage was strong, rigid, unwilling to move. I bounced from him, preparing to land backward on the floor, when his strong arms reached for me.

My face was now pressed against his chest as cologne radiated from his skin that made my head spin with lust. Jax lacked the mature and distinguished composure that the mysterious stranger at the lake had.

Through his shirt I could feel his heart pounding. His slow, controlled breathing caused his chest to expand, and each muscle rippled, one by one. I glanced up at Jax to find he had removed his mask. His piercing blue eyes were staring directly at me, his complexion irresistibly smooth.

I gasped as I looked at him, while his arrogant smirk pulled his lips into a bigger smile. "I was getting too hot." The white mask fell on the ground at our feet as he shrugged off his shirt.

"Tell me, Cassidy, do you feel that?" he asked, placing my hand on his bare chest.

My breath caught as my fingertips stilled at the thrum of his pounding heart, as though it was going to leap out of his chest at any moment.

I slowly nodded my head, unsure what to say, or what would happen next.

"Cassidy," he purred, tilting my chin up to face him, his eyes staring into mine.

The butterflies were buzzing with energy, and my stomach twisted as their wings fluttered uncontrollably.

I felt my heart thump in sync with his. We stood there, staring at each other, neither of us moving, not wanting to break this moment. His hand drew up to the side of my face, as his fingers stroked my curls, and his lips inched closer to mine.

In my peripheral vision, fireflies hovered in the air, casting their beads of orange light against our skin like a miniature disco ball, as our hearts beat to their own melody. Maybe it would not be so bad, settling down, starting a family. I pondered a bonded life; one I did not expect or desire. But now, it made sense. As I stared into his blue eyes, I was lost. *Why am I feeling sad about being bonded to Jax? There are worse people Fate could have matched me with. Yet I still longed for the stranger at the lake. How can I give Jax my heart and soul when both are also connected to that mysterious man? Would I see that man tonight? Or is he avoiding me?*

Just then I caught the familiar scent, the one I had smelled by the lake. My mind grew fuzzy as I tried to pinpoint the culprit. There was a clear distinction between the two masculine fragrances that assaulted my nostrils and filled my head with lust. I inhaled deeply. It was stronger, more earthy, and more mature than Jax's, but their scents stirred something inside of me.

As I stared into Jax's eyes, his lips lightly brushed against mine, I envisioned the other man's face, the stranger from the lake. Comparing them both, I recalled how his stubble had tickled my face, unlike the smooth baby face of Jax's.

When Jax kissed me, it was light and timid; I yearned for the fierce, fiery passion of the stranger.

Jax's confidence grew as I surrendered to him, allowing his hands to explore my body stopping at the small of my back. His grip was firm as his tongue sought mine. "Cassidy," he murmured.

His hand hovered over my breast, his fingertips lightly resting on top of the corset. "You're beautiful," he whispered. His member throbbed against my crotch, as his need was building. My resolve slipped; my mind wiped of all thoughts. All of my feelings faded for the stranger by the lake. My body melted into Jax's touch.

A growl sliced through my empty mind, and it demanded my attention. My eyes snapped open.

"*Mate,*" *it snarled.* This was Flynn's codeword. *He needs me.*

I backed away from Jax. "I... I must-" My eyes calculated the escape plan. "I'm sorry..."

"Cassidy?" Jax's face frowned, showing concern. "What is wrong?" His big blue eyes opened wide in shock, and his brow knitted together in confusion.

My feet pounded quickly in the direction we had just come, barging through the double doors, and shoving my way through the crowds that now lingered on the dance-floor.

"*Mate!*" his voice called again. He felt close. My heart pounded.

Honing in on his internal voice, I navigated by twisting through corridors, feeling as though I was running in circles inside this labyrinth of a castle, until I reached the origin of the voice. I placed my hands on the two heavy oak double doors. A light thrum vibrated through my fingertips. The doors had their own pulse. With all my might, I pushed against them, thinking he must be inside. My breath caught in my throat. The room was cast in total darkness.

"Flynn?" I called out, my voice echoing in the vast emptiness. "Flynn, are you in here?"

Jax's rejected and hurt face lingered in my mind. When I fumbled for a light switch, my mind was still frantically trying to reach out to Flynn, alarmed by his use of our codeword. It was only to be used if his secret was about to be revealed. *I am sure I followed him to the correct place, but why would he be here in the dark? Why isn't he answering me?*

My breath was getting trapped in my chest, rattling, and wheezing as if my lungs restricted, and my ribs crushed them. Panic kicked in. "Flynn!" I called out.

"*Cassidy?*" His voice was frightened inside my mind.

"*What's wrong? Where are you?*" I tried to find the light switch. When my fingers stumbled upon it, the weight of my anxiety lifted from my chest. The hum of the light reverberated overhead. There was a loud static buzzing, and then the lights flickered back to life.

"You called me, didn't you?" I asked him telepathically. *"I thought I heard... Do you need me?"* I gasped in relief upon hearing his voice.

"No, I'm fine, Cass. Where did you go with Jax?" Flynn asked.

My jaw dropped and my eyes widened as all of my other thoughts had evaporated like smoke. I was not alone, but it was not Flynn who was before me.

Two large golden oversized thrones sat in the center of the room, intricately decorated with swirls, adorned with gems and scarlet-colored upholstery. I was in the sacred room that no one other than the King and his counsel were allowed to enter. Only one of them was empty, and the other was occupied. Dark brown eyes bore into mine, reaching inside my head. A small smile flitted across his lips as he leaned forward in the chair. His legs splayed, and an elbow rested on each knee. A black half-face mask was carefully positioned in front of his eyes, partially shielding it from my view.

"I wondered how long it would take you to come." He purred, his hand slowly letting the mask fall to the floor.

My breath caught in my throat as the blood in my veins turned to ice. His alluring scent held me rooted to the spot. It was the stranger from the lake.

FIVE

Flynn

I took in our dark and dusty surroundings in a small, secret space that Jace had found. It was a storage cupboard of some sort, hidden and away from the party. Like the pied piper he lured me here. My dirty and grimy hand fell from the wall. Fitting, really, considering that was how our love was viewed. *We should not be here. I should be looking for Cassidy, not here with him.*

As I looked down into Jace's eyes, I could feel her calling me, but my reluctance to stop Jace held me rooted to the spot. He was kneeling before me, hungry with desire. As he stared back at me, his hands lingered on the waistband of my suit trousers.

"Not now," I grimaced, stepping away from him, watching his hands fall to his sides. My legs felt too weak to move, but I forced them to take several steps back.

Our illicit deeds grew more intense with each encounter. We were becoming too reckless. Yet the thought of his lips on me made me ache with desire. *But it is forbidden.* I told myself. *Our love will never be allowed.*

"Flynn..." Jace sighed, slowly getting to his feet. "We may never get such a secluded, *opportune* moment again." His hand cupped my face, pulling me into a kiss. My resolve was fading. Then his hand reached lower beneath my waistband, wrapping around my length.

I gasped at the shock of his touch, so firm yet so tender. He stroked my length as our lips crashed against each other. *This must stop,* I kept telling myself as I leaned back against the door. His hand movements grew more forceful, more determined.

"Jace," I gasped as I felt him lower himself once more. His hot breath was near the base of my shaft.

"Jace, we should... we should stop..." but despite my words, my body did not want this to end. The sensation of his lips enveloping my manhood, his hands cupping my scrotum, gently massaging them as he took my full length in his mouth made me weak.

"Fuck," I gasped, my hands clutching at his hair.

This is the farthest we have ever been. Playing it safe had sufficed previously, yet now I craved more. We both needed more.

"I want you," he murmured, his tongue teased my tip. "I need you."

A growl escaped me, and upon hearing his words, my emotions swirled like a tornado as I pulled him to his feet. Pressing him against the wall, my mouth frantically planted hot, passionate kisses on his lips.

"I. Want. You. Too." I moaned, as my hand slid down his torso. My fingers were in a frantic search for his shaft. Hastily unzipping his trousers, my hands trembled. *This is it,* I thought. *This is where I sign my death wish.*

"Flynn, where are you?" Cassidy's voice was frantic. It caught me off guard. The desire, lust, and hunger all evaporated in an instant.

Jace looked at me, panting, his face questioning. "Flynn, what's wrong?"

My member was now limp. Stepping away from him, I adjusted my tie, and combed my fingers through my hair, trying to flatten it.

Once again, her voice echoed in my head, *"Flynn?"*

Is she in danger? In my frenzied state, I had shut out her thoughts. I gritted my teeth, skulking away from Jace, angry with myself for being so selfish.

"Cass?" I asked her, trying to keep my breathlessness out of my mental voice. *"What's wrong?"*

Jace looked at me, his face showing understanding. "It's okay," he whispered, planting a soft kiss on my cheek. "There will be other times." He sighed, his hand interlocking with mine.

I nodded once, clenching my jaw. Whispering, I apologized and rubbed the back of his hand with my thumb. "I..."

He placed his finger to my lips, shaking his head. "One day, this won't be wrong." I brought his hand up to my lips, and kissed it lightly. "One day, we won't have the threat of execution over our heads."

He smiled, slowly retracting his hand from mine. "But that would remove the fun." He winked, and then he left the closet. I watched him leave in silence, regretting my lack of control.

"Cass?" I called out to her. *"Where are you?"*

SIX

Cassidy

The walls seemed to close in on me as I stood paralyzed before him. My heart hammered in my chest. I returned his stare. It was deep and intense, reflecting his persona.

"Welcome to my castle." His voice echoed. "I am Logan. *Prince* Logan."

"It... was you?" My voice was unsteady, cracking in parts. "How did you..." *How could he reach into my mind? How could he trick me into believing he was Flynn? How did he know the codeword? Can he-*

"Yes. I can read your thoughts." He purred.

Unwilling to move, yet feeling as if I was being pulled to him by an invisible cowboy lasso, I was now less than a foot from him. The Earthy, masculine scent permeated my every thought. Images of our kiss flashed through my head. My desire burned hot within my core.

He growled. A low, deep guttural sound, which resonated from his chest rather than his throat.

He leaned forward and tugged at my wrists, using my shock to his advantage. The momentum brought me closer to him, until I stood between his spread legs, both my wrists held in his hand.

"I can smell him on you," he barked, pulling me down to him, his mouth close to my neck. His breath burned as it flitted over my skin. Goosebumps pricked my skin. "Did the two of you..."

"No!" I roared, offended by his tone.

I yanked my hands, trying to free them from his grasp, but his grip held firm. His other hand held the side of my head, entangling his fingers among my curls. He brought my face closer to his. I gulped.

It was rude to interrupt royalty when they spoke. "I'm sorry...*sir*, I-" I gasped. "I mean, my *Prince*," I added quickly. My eyes dropped to the floor as my body succumbed to his dominance.

His chuckle sent chills down my spine, and goosebumps returned to my flesh. "Formalities are not required when we are alone, Cassidy," he murmured. His legs moved as his feet slipped between mine. I was suddenly swept off of them, as my weight crashed down on his lap. I straddled him, on the throne. Blasphemy at its finest.

His lips brushed against the base of my throat, slow, and perfectly timed as he worked his way up to my jawline.

His shaft was solid against my groin, and it throbbed beneath my weight. I felt my core moisten in lustful anticipation. His lips were suddenly on mine, his grasp of my wrists relinquished. I knew I was free to move away, if I so desired, but instead my arms snaked around his neck, and my body pressed firmly against his as I deepened the kiss. My hips thrashed against his.

His soft moan caught me by surprise, inflicting a slight smile upon my lips.

"Cassidy...you are driving me crazy," he purred. Breaking from the kiss, his eyes bore into mine. "You are all I have thought about..." he whimpered, his voice low and quiet. "You are mine."

My insides melted at the thought of his lust for me. *Is this why he shied away from the party?*

"Yes," his voice hissed, pressing his forehead against mine. His breath was hot against my face.

"How did you do that... how can you reach my mind?" I asked him telepathically.

His manhood stirred once more, poking my heat as if stoking embers to reignite the fire that burned within me. *"I thought only those who were bonded could... you know, do this."*

"Do you not communicate with him like that... Flynn, is it?" His mental voice cooed, as his fingers fiddled with the satin bow that tied the bodice to my dress. *"Wasn't he who you thought I was?"*

I nodded slowly, biting my lip as I felt my top loosen. I should have heard the difference in their mental voices, the dulcet tones of the eldest prince before me.

"Why have you promised yourself to Flynn, when he is not your mate?" he growled, each breath ragged and hot against my face. "We both know you both don't belong together *in that way*. He has no desire for you like I have." His eyes penetrated mine.

Logan knows the truth.

His fingers clawed at the satin loops of the corset, loosening each strand, "You should know I forbid it..." his lips grazing my collarbone. "You. Are. Mine." The bodice fell away from my torso, exposing my bare chest to him. "I *want you* to be all mine."

His hand cupped my breast, and as he drew his mouth to my nipple, his hot touch tickled the sensitive skin around it. My back arched instinctively as my heat thrashed against his member. *Fuck, is this really happening? Am I about to consummate this bond between us?*

A moan escaped my lips as his mouth flitted from one nipple to the other. Logan chuckled, "We are not going all the way *just yet*."

"*Cassidy?*" Flynn's voice pierced my mind. "*What is going on? Have you...with Jax?*"

"*She is not with Jax, she is with me. Prince Logan,*" He growled telepathically. "Cassidy will be *mine, not his*."

His mouth suctioned over my nipple. I cried out from the sensation. My body had a mind of its own as my hungry core thrashed against his solid shaft. A tingling sensation rippled against my shielded clit.

"No, she will be mine." Jax's voice reverberated. The door flew open behind me as the hinges creaked in protest as they swung wide to allow him to enter the room.

Logan's body stilled, and my breast fell from his mouth.

"Jax!" I gasped, my hands instinctively wrapping around my bare bosom. I tried to get up as my head was spinning. Delirious with lust, I was confused by all of their presences in my mind. Before I could move, Jax was behind me. His hands covered mine, and his mouth was against my neck.

I felt Logan's hands slide underneath my dress, tickling the inside of my thighs before his fingertips brushed gently against my slit, his mouth covering my own to suppress my gasp.

Jax's hands pried mine away, replacing them. My nipples were as hard as bullets against his palms as Logan's fingers slid inside me. Slow at first, but building with pace. My heart pounded in my ear matching the rhythm of his fingers. As a ripple of pleasure washed over me, I felt the two brothers' bodies tense.

"Fuck," I gasped, my hands clawed the arms of the throne as my body writhed under their touch.

"My turn," Jax's voice cut over my moan. His strong arms lifted me away from Logan, and he placed me on the empty throne beside him.

My body longed for Logan's presence, but he sat there watching us. His eyes studied the scene, as Jax lowered himself to his knees, pulling my legs over the arms of the throne, spreading my heat as wide as he could. His hand disappeared under the skirt of my dress, and then his head followed. When I felt his breath on my sensitive folds, I was on the edge again.

The moment his tongue curled along my crease all of my inhibitions faded away. There was nothing else I wanted at that moment, other than my sweet release. I felt pleasure building inside of me, wanting to explode once more.

As Jax's mouth clamped over my clit and his fingers thrust inside my core, my eyes locked onto Logan. His hand was wrapped around his shaft as he pounded it in rhythm with Jax's fingers. He moaned softly as his eyes fixated on the scene before him.

"Cassidy, what the hell is going on?" Flynn's voice panicked in my mind. Snapping me out of this reverie. My eyes opened wide with surprise. The scene before me was so surreal. It had to be a dream.

"She is getting a glimpse of the future. If she chooses the right brother!" Jax's mental voice responded as he slipped in another finger, his tongue lapping at my sensitive nub.

My hand sought something to grasp as a powerful orgasm overcame me.

Without hesitation, Logan was there, his shaft in my hand. It was thick and long, much bigger than I had expected. His smirk grew as he discovered my surprise in our thoughts. I stroked its length, my grip firm, moving my hand in time to Jax's fingers as they entered me.

"Faster," he demanded. "Harder."

I could barely contain my moans as wave after wave of pleasure crashed through my body, writhing, and bucking against his tongue. Logan curled his hands in my hair, pulling my lips to his shaft. My eyes widened as it entered my mouth. I teased the tip with my tongue, feeling it twitch, hearing his groan as I tried to swallow his full length, easing it in my mouth inch by inch. Sucking harder with each thrust, I felt another orgasm nearing, as Jax continued to devour my heat, pumping his fingers frantically inside me.

"I need her," Jax's voice purred, as he slid out from under my dress.

"No!" Logan's voice bellowed, silencing him. "Only once she has chosen one of us." His eyes narrowed, and his mouth parted as his breathing quickened. My mouth took his length up to the hilt.

"Do I have to choose?" I asked selfishly, my mind too full, needing to reach my climax to concentrate fully.

"Not now Cassidy, but you will need to make a choice," Logan panted before he gasped aloud. "Fuck, you're good."

Jax seethed in jealousy, as he stood on the other side of me, his shaft expecting the same treatment.

Logan nodded his head, slowly stepping away from me. "I will show you how a *man* satisfies a woman."

Wasting no time, Logan buried his face between my thighs, his tongue slowly teasing my nub. Thrusting two fingers inside me, I cried out, muffled by Jax's member now lodged inside my mouth. He grunted, heavy and loud. Tangling his hand in my hair, using my head to control the pace and the depth.

I could not think of anything other than the feeling of being full. They penetrated my mouth and my slit. My desire went beyond just their fingers. I wanted Jax's boyish energy pounding at my flesh. while at the same time I craved Logan's huge shaft deep inside me. *How am I supposed to choose? I was attracted to them both. I wanted them both.*

As my climax erupted, I screamed out loud. The sounds of my pleasure echoed in the otherwise silent room.

"That's a good girl, Cass, come for me," Logan purred, his tongue sliding inside my tight entrance, inflicting a small squeal to come from my mouth. Just as another wave came, my muscles convulsed, and my body rocked as the orgasm ripped through my body, shattering any remaining thoughts I had.

"Cassidy!" Jax called as his member throbbed. A jet of warm, sticky fluid trickled down my throat. "Fuck!" he moaned as I swallowed, milking him until he had nothing else left to give.

Logan paused. *"That was not part of the deal,"* his internal voice sniped at his brother.

Jax shrugged, a lazy, satisfied grin on his face as he fastened his pants.

Logan was on his feet, leaving my slit lonely and empty.

Wiping my lip with the back of my hand, I reached for him. "Do you want to come too?" I asked, guiding his member to my mouth, "Come for me, *Prince Logan*," I murmured, my hand working against his length. His groans of pleasure were like music to my ears. All I had wanted to do was please them, to enjoy them both and to be enjoyed by them.

Within moments his manhood jerked, thrusting deep inside my mouth, the tip touching the back of my throat as his hot seed erupted from the tip, sliding down the back of my throat, staying like that until every drop was secreted.

"Cassidy. You can only have one of us." Logan's voice huffed as his body shuddered. "You will have one month to decide." Shoving his limp shaft back into his trousers, Logan said, "This will never happen again." His mouth crashed against mine, one final time before they both left me alone, reveling in the aftermath of my pleasure.

What the fuck just happened?

SEVEN

The countdown is on. Logan and I had one month to convince Cassidy to choose one of us. We needed to explore our bonds without consummation. Neither one of us liked the idea of the other being with her. Sharing was not our strong suit.

In that one evening, any brotherly affection we had toward each other had disintegrated, disappearing faster than my load down her throat.

From that shared night with Cassidy, an intolerable fracture had formed between us. It was too immeasurable, to ignore. The tension was palpable. Cassidy had caused a crack in our brotherly bond and our loyalty of blood and family ties.

It doesn't matter, I told myself stubbornly. *She will choose me.* I envisioned ruling the Kingdom with her by my side. *But what would happen to him?* I knew he would always have a connection with her, even if our bond was sealed with our intimate act. She would always be attracted to him. *He would have to be banished from the kingdom. No, better yet, he will need to be removed from Xeyiera for good. Only when Logan is gone by the finality of death would Cassidy's heart be solely mine.*

"Jax? What will you do?" My twin, Demi, was suddenly in my room.

It was the morning after The Masquerade of Whispers and short of eight hours since Cassidy had made the throne room vibrate in her cries of delight, and less than seven hours since she had left the palace. Despite my hatred about her attraction to Logan, my heart and groin longed for her. It felt more like years than mere hours without Cassidy's presence. I shrugged. *A lot can change in one month. She will grow bored of Logan's stoic manner.*

I had struggled to sleep, my mind and my member keeping me awake with thoughts of things I wanted to do to her. Those acts that were forbidden until she had chosen me. They were all playing in my mind like a pornographic movie. No woman had ever made me that hard. I have dabbled with my fair share of girls, but there was something more, a deeper connection with Cassidy.

It was not lust that had initially attracted me to her, it was like an unseen force that drew me to her. Everything and everyone faded into nothingness, she was the sole occupier of my attention, the only person that mattered. Being alone with her in the courtyard, feeling the way our hearts began to beat in perfect synchrony, I knew she was the one I had been searching for; the woman I was destined to be with. *Cassidy is my soulmate. I want to make her mine. Forever.*

"You should visit her." Demi's voice echoed as she entered my room.

I smirked recalling the conversation I had with Cassidy. Unbeknownst to her, I could have a telepathic link with anyone if I wanted, not just my pretend twin, Demi.

Demi's eyes twinkled, clearly enjoying reliving my memories too. "Don't worry. I'm team Jax." She giggled. "You should be the first person she sees after what happened last night. You know, to re-jog her memory." Demi winked at me.

She had a point. Perhaps it may not be only Cassidy's decision to make. The people of the Kingdom will want a say about their next King. Perhaps I needed to win them over, too.

"Demi, send a messenger. Tell them to bring Cassidy to me. I will wait for her in the library... Oh, keep Logan busy too!" I called out to her.

With a nod and a smile of pure excitement, she left. I grimaced a little, knowing I had just given her free rein to create mischief.

What was taking so long? Two hours had passed, Demi had not yet returned and Cassidy was not here either. *No one keeps me waiting.*

Pacing the castle alone had given me time to think, to ponder the future, should she choose me. I considered what changes I would make when I became King. For years, I believed I would never have a chance on the throne unless my brother died without an heir.

As a Royal Prince, I commanded respect, but I was grateful for the lack of watchful eyes marking my every move. I could bend the rules without consequences. A part of me did not want to be King. I yearned for the liberty to travel, unrestricted by the obligations of being a King. Another part of me resented Logan; the shadow he cast left a bitter taste in my mouth.

Cassidy. The thought of her made me smile: her petite waist that accentuated her delicious and curvaceous ass, the delicate porcelain skin of her bosom and the plump, juicy lips that formed her innocent smile. My longing for her was driving me insane as I recalled her soft skin, and the feel of her breasts in my hands. I remembered the taste of her and the sensation of my tongue as it buried deep inside her slit. *I needed her to choose me.*

An unseen force drew my eyes in her direction the moment she stepped into the hall last night. A pull to her far greater than that of just lust, I was aware of her every movement, my senses heightened as her alluring scent enticed me from across the room. My eyes scanned her black lace dress, the corset hugging her hourglass figure and accentuated her cleavage, looking both sexy and elegant. I knew I had to have her. *Fuck Logan, she is mine.*

Dancing with her was like nothing I had experienced. She enchanted me, making me feel that we were the sole occupants of the room, the way her body responded to mine demonstrated that she too could feel the connection between us. Yet it was only as we entered the courtyard that I received his angry warning.

"Back off," Logan said. *"She's mine."*

The Royal family was gifted with the ability of telepathy from the Elders. It was how Logan had sent his warning, and it was how we were able to reach into Cassidy's mind without consummating a bond.

Logan had invaded my thoughts, used me as his eyes, unwilling to join in the party, skulking in the throne room, waiting for her to find him. Instead, she was with me.

I saw him scowl and sulk. Though he could not deny it, he must have felt the magnetic pull Cassidy had on us both.

"She must choose," he said that night. *"Neither of us can force her decision. We will not consummate until she has made her choice."*

When I released my load in her mouth, it had not been on purpose. She worked me into a frenzy and took me beyond my self-restraint. I lost my mind, and I had lost control of my body, losing my load faster than I ever could have imagined possible.

Just thinking about her moans of ecstasy, her whimpers of unadulterated pleasure made my member hard. *I want her. I need her. Now.* I needed to bring myself to release, and fast. A quick one, before she turned up. I needed to make her beg for it. *And beg for it, she will.*

I had crossed a line. I had disobeyed Logan and broken the pact we made before our tryst ensued. By secreting my seed in her mouth first, I had started a rivalry between us, one that threatened to destroy our family, and our kingdom.

I have started a war.

EIGHT

Logan

I knew where I could find her. A place where we could be alone.

That one place I had found her, but only because her scent had caught my attention. I did not go out intending to find *the one*. Now I was here, waiting for her, hoping she would listen to my plea to meet me here.

"Just to talk," I told her in my mind, although I hoped for more than that.

For ten minutes, I watched the breeze ripple across the water. I relived moments from last night, trying to focus solely on Cassidy and her enjoyment, but then jealousy swelled in my chest like an angry, possessive beast. *Seeing Jax's hands glide along her body and his lips pressed against hers, while their shared moments of intimacy and the flush in her cheeks—*

A sharp pain sliced my chest in the sudden realization that for the first time in my life, I was vulnerable, exposed to a future I had no control over. *What if she doesn't choose me?*

Taking several deep breaths, I tried to suppress the flicker of doubt that had manifested in my mind. Instead, I forced myself to focus on my adoration of Cassidy. I smiled recalling how I savored every one of her sweet, tentative kisses. Then there was the flicker of confusion that swept across her face as we both connected with her telepathically. The way her delicious moans of pleasure escaped her lips while we took her to the precipice of her climax made my shaft harden and my heart race.

Jax had crossed a line, though. He disobeyed me when I had been generous enough to share her delights for one evening. *I won't let it happen again.* If he could easily defy my command, he would never respect me as King, or accept her decision if she chose me.

Their connection, and their chemistry, were undeniable, but ours was stronger. Even though she was out of my reach, beyond the lake, her scent lingered in the air, teasing my senses. I could taste her. Her attraction was like metal filings to a magnet. She was drawn to me as much as I was to her. *We will be together.*

"Logan?" Cassidy's voice was weak as it drifted across the lake. "You wanted to talk?" I could tell even from this distance, she was exhausted.

Is she still recovering from last night? I thought as I slowly approached her. My eyes fixated on Cassidy as we both approached one another, both of us stopping a few feet apart. I recognized the tree beside us, the very spot I had pinned her, where we kissed and ground against each other only a few days ago. A smile flickered across my face as I recalled that memory.

"If that's your desire. I have brought us a picnic." I pointed to a spot behind me, shaded by a weeping willow tree. Her eyes sparkled. A large plaid blanket laid on the ground with a wicker picnic basket sat in the middle. Her smile could light up the darkest of places.

"I was unsure if girls like picnics," I confessed, feeling self-conscious.

"Well, I'm not like most girls." She smiled; her hand automatically slipped into mine. "And I love picnics."

I felt my shoulders relax as relief washed over me.

"So about yesterday..." she started, as she sat down, her face showing her awkwardness,

"We don't have to talk about that now," I said, trying to busy myself by pulling out a chilled bottle of champagne, one that had been left from the ball. I got two flute glasses and began pouring the drink. "We can talk about other things, if you'd like," I said, as I handed her the glass.

"Okay. Tell me more about you, Logan. I mean, Prince Logan," Cassidy said, flirtatiously.

"When it is just us, you do not need to use the formalities. I am just Logan," I said. She nodded her head, taking a small sip from her glass.

"Um, there isn't much that you don't already know," I replied, my tone light. "My coffee preference is black with just one sugar. I prefer my whiskey neat with ice, and I am rather partial to watermelons." A smile spread across my face as I reached into my bag and triumphantly revealed slices of refreshing watermelon, a tangible demonstration of my point.

"Did your servants prepare this?" she asked, before lifting a slice up to her mouth.

I could not help but watch her mouth move as she took small nibbles of the fruit. Fascinated by her lips, I could not stop dreaming about them. I imagined her lips against mine, remembering how good they felt against the base of my shaft.

"Ahem...So... did they?" she asked, snapping me out of my trance.

I shook my head. Picking up my slice of watermelon, I gently nuzzled it as if it was her slit. Her cheeks blushed a deep red hue.

So, I am not the only one still reliving the memories then, I thought. "I can fend for myself," I told her. "They are called attentive staff, by the way, and they are very well-paid members of society."

She nodded, the smile still playing on her lips. I wanted to reach out and kiss her. "Tell me Cassidy, what are your aspirations? Are you going to take over your father in the artillery industry?"

"Oh, God. No," she blurted, quickly covering her mouth, her eyes wide in horror. "I mean, what he does is very important, but it's not what I want to be doing for the rest of my life."

"What is?" I asked. Our hands touched as we reached for another slice. Her touch sent ripples through me, like small electrical currents.

Her eyes snapped up at mine before retracting her hand. "I want to be a healer," she said matter-of-factly. "My mom is a midwife. Actually, she is Estoria's leading midwife."

I pushed the plate of watermelon slices towards her after taking another slice. "So, you will not follow in her footsteps?"

She shook her head, seeming to contemplate what slice she should take.

"Oh, how come?" I asked. "It's awe-inspiring to see a child being born, but also terrifying. I remembered being there for Jax and Demi's births and how I fetched clean towels and their blankets. A few hands were available to assist to stop the bleeding. All the midwives were trying their best. I had also offered to help, though my actions were in vain. My mother had lost too much blood."

"I'm sorry about your mom," she blurted, her hand resting on mine. Even though heat emanated from it, a sudden coolness washed through me. It was a soothing relief that had almost wiped my sadness away. "I can't imagine how hard it must have been, growing up without your mother," she whispered, her hand smoothing the back of my palm. "Mother said one of her deepest regrets was that she was not able to help the Queen."

When I ate a chunk of watermelon, it felt like it was made from razor blades, the way it cut my throat as I swallowed it.

Cassidy's fingers traced the side of my face, "Logan..."

"You don't need to make your choice yet," I told her, our eyes locked. I felt myself slip into the vibrant green depths of hers, losing all other trails of thought. "I hope you choose me, Cassidy." I blurted out loud.

We were sitting, innocently eating watermelon, and talking, but then all it took was one look of desire. Her eyes twinkled, and the fire lit inside of me. In one fluid motion she was beneath me, as I pinned her to the blanket.

A squeal of delight escaped her lips before I silenced her with an intense kiss. Her clothes came off as if I was unpeeling each layer of her innocence, until her naked body molded to mine. She writhed beneath me, her heat pressing against my shaft, causing me to abandon all thoughts of the picnic.

NINE

Cassidy

I woke up sore. My head was pounding, my legs ached and my core throbbed. I was confused with memories from the night before.

It seemed so surreal, yet so predictable. I knew there was a reason for my dread. My reluctance to attend the Masquerade of Whispers had been justified. My gut told me that my attendance would seal my Fate, and low and behold, it had been right. Never in a million years did I expect to be bound to both Princes.

Logan and Jax both wanted me. As the words formed in my mind, and I attempted to convey them to Flynn in less vivid detail, the entire thing still felt unbelievable. I knew he would uncover the explicit memories; it was only a matter of time.

Embarrassed, not wanting my best friend to see such intimate and personal scenes, I tried not to recall those moments or relive their kisses, hands all over my body, and tongues in places no other had been. I tried to forget how they both made me feel. Those were moments of pure self-indulgent bliss, and I enjoyed the sensations that thrummed within every fiber of my being. I yearned to experience that rush of pleasure again and again.

My mind turned to the important matter. It had kept me fretting all night. *Who am I going to choose?* I anticipated the decision would not be easy. Not only physically attracted to both, but my soul also felt torn between them. My heart was being simultaneously drawn in their separate directions. It was as if Fate was still undecided to whom I would belong.

I felt like a science experiment we completed when I was in middle school. We had to lure metal filings to our magnet at one end as our partner tried to entice them with their magnetism at the other. Like the metal filings, my heart was torn between the two magnets that were the princes. I quivered at my indecisiveness.

My head and my heart were not in sync. Still, I hesitated to commit and settle down. I desired that taste of freedom, to explore beyond Estoria, beyond Eyre. I did not wish for my wings to be clipped so early in my adult life.

A wave of resentment at both my parents surged through me; they had forced me to attend that ball. Though I knew deep down, I could not pin the full blame on them. The loathing I had for the Rules of Conduct was even greater than the impending threat of punishment, should one disobey direct orders. The invitation to the Masquerade of Whispers was nothing more than an order from the second highest governing body of Eyre; the Royal Family.

Though it was not explicitly stated, my attendance was made mandatory by including this one small sentence: *"It is with their utmost insistence that Cassidy be present on this night."* Nothing would have excused me from attending. The Royal's orders were only superseded by those of the Elders. They were the ones I could thank for this scenario. It was to them whom I directed most of my hatred.

"Cass, this is an enormous deal," Flynn gasped. I rolled my eyes as I communicated with him mentally. *"Whoever you choose, they will be the one who is King..."*

"Yeah." I sighed, slowly sitting upright in my bed. My recollection of getting home was hazy after my picnic with Logan. The sun was too bright for my tired eyes. *"Flynn, I only have one month to make that decision,"* I added. Leaning back against the metal headboard, enjoying the coldness of the metal, it felt soothing against my spine.

"Cassidy, this decision goes beyond your personal desires," he pointed out. *"The individual you select will govern all of us."*

"I know," I retorted, biting at my fingernail., *"and I don't know either of them...properly."* I sighed. *"Flynn, what am I going to do?"*

"You need to consider this carefully..." He fell silent, his mind churning. Then he seemed to disappear momentarily.

"What if I choose the wrong one?" I asked. *What if whoever I choose turns out to be a dreadful King?*

"Cass, you cannot choose the wrong one." His voice was firm, full of concern. *"Do not simply choose based on your attraction. You must also choose who you believe will make the best King."*

I spent most of the morning avoiding my family, wanting to steer clear of the expectant glare of Father, the concerned look of Mother, and the awe-struck gaze of my sister. Of course, it was common knowledge that I had been seen disappearing with Jax Silverthorne. Countless people likely shared such juicy gossip. The whispers did not know, not yet, that Jax wasn't the only one I was with that evening. Their sole preoccupation was why an announcement of our bond or his coronation as King hadn't been made yet.

Logan's voice broke through my thoughts, expressing his disapproval of the announcement. It was serious, stern. *"I want you to choose me,"* he brooded.

I felt my heart flutter. Just hearing his voice, it appeared, had an effect on me.

"Meet me, by the lake, in twenty minutes. We can talk." He did not wait for me to respond; it was clear his instruction was an order, not a question.

Shit. I thundered through my wardrobe, looking for something other than the gray joggers and a baggy t-shirt to wear. Finally, I decided on a pair of black jeans and a cropped t-shirt that showed off a sliver of my toned midriff. When I left the house, heading for my secret sanctuary, I could not help but feel excited and apprehensive at the thought of seeing him again. Logan Silverthorne, the oldest Prince, the traditional choice to be the next heir to the throne, wanted *me.*

Choosing him to rule as King made sense. It was his birthright, his life's purpose. Yet, aside from all those logical reasons, I still knew nothing about him, aside from his ability to make my pulse race and my knees weak. He claimed he wanted to talk.

"Just talk? Yeah, right..." Flynn chuckled, amused by mine and Logan's exchange. *"You better not forget to wear matching underwear then!"* he laughed before I shut him out.

I left the house, concentrating on the simple act of walking and distracting my thoughts by counting each step. I pondered my life's transformation. Only a few days ago, my sanctuary was my quiet haven, the only place I could be alone. Flynn and Logan were now aware of its location, and it was not my safe space anymore. There was nowhere I could call my own. My thoughts were not safe anymore.

How are they able to access my mind? To communicate telepathically? I pushed deeper into the borough of Fic. It was almost lunchtime; the factories were busy churning out thick plumes of smokes as they produced items on a mass scale. The loud thrum of machinery beyond their walls was deafening.

The large brick boundary came into my vision. For most of my life, I communicated with Flynn telepathically, and I wondered how that was possible.

As young children, we saw our connection as something cool and innocent. Communicating with him like this had made it easier for us to navigate our mischief without consequences. In school, this ability proved beneficial, particularly during tests, as it allowed us to share answers and clarify questions. In our early teens, the connection aided us in sneaking out after curfew. We would bend the rules.

My heart skipped a beat when I realized my best friend might be my soulmate. Flynn was not just a nice guy, but he knew everything about me. Plus, he was handsome. He had a cute boy-band look with his floppy sandy-brown hair, pale blue-gray eyes, and unblemished skin. He maintained a regular workout routine that sculpted his muscular physique. It was not surprising he turned heads, and it had not surprised me that his good looks attracted Princess Demi, whose existence I did not know about until the Masquerade of Whispers.

Part of me still wished I held onto that hope that we would be together, despite the knowledge that he did not find me, or any female, attractive. It certainly would have made my life much easier.

As I sat before Logan, I could not help but wonder: *how can I get to know him? What sort of questions do I ask? How does he take his coffee? What's his favorite drink? His favorite color? Does he have a favorite fruit?* They all seemed like petty questions in the grand scheme of things. He had answered them anyway, the telltale smirk played across his face that he had been reading my thoughts.

He took a bite of his watermelon, his lips wrapping around the soft flesh reminiscent of him lapping at my core. I blushed as another ripple of desire flooded me, my core throbbing. I needed to feel his tongue there once again. I tried not to watch him, not to imagine his lips working on my slit rather than the slice of exotic fruit, but my brain was sex-addled, full of lust and desire for him. *Of course, I can't just talk to him.* I thought with a sigh.

I squirmed as a fierce fire ignited within. A light flashed across his eyes as his body lunged towards me. His wrists pinning mine down on the blanket, firm and unyielding. The sudden movement had caught me off guard as a squeal escaped my lips.

My lips desperately sought his, as my body succumbed to his dominance and his solid member pressed against my thigh. I tasted the sweet watermelon on his breath, mixed with mint from his toothpaste. His scent, musky and masculine, filled my nostrils, sending my brain into a meltdown. He, and his body, were all I wanted. There were no other thoughts circling my head other than my craving of him. My wish was for him to take me to cloud nine once more.

His hands slid under my top, cupping my breasts, before sliding my top gracefully over my head. His eyes widened when he caught sight of my emerald green bra. "Did you already know green was my favorite color?" he murmured, laying me on my back so he could kiss along my neck, trailing his tongue between the crease of my cleavage, before freeing my breasts one at a time.

Taking his time, his tongue slowly flicked over one nipple, then the other. My back arched instinctively. A gasp escaped my lips. My heart pounded against my ribs. Within moments he was kissing along my abdomen, stopping when he reached the waistband of my jeans, not hesitating to undo them and rip them off my legs in one easy sweep. My matching green laced thong was now fully exposed to him. A damp patch was visible from my arousal.

He lowered his lips to kiss me once more before removing them, delicately rolling his tongue along the inner folds, hovering tentatively over my nub. A slight graze of his tongue against it sent a forceful shockwave through my body. His name rolled off my tongue instinctively in my moan of delight.

"Say it again," he urged, thrusting his fingers inside me. His voice was gritty and animalistic in his desire. His lips encircled my clit forming a perfect seal. My hands clutched at his short hair, holding him there as my first orgasm rocked my body. I panted his name as my core throbbed around his fingers. His tongue was quick to lap up my nectar as it flowed uncontrollably.

He was suddenly shirtless, unzipping his own jeans, before laying on his back. "Sit on my face," he commanded. My eyes opened wide, but my heart hammered in my chest as warmth flooded my core. The risk of being caught out in the open turned me on. *What if someone saw us?*

"It is not a request" he purred, pulling my mouth towards him. "Your future King demands to eat your deliciousness." His tongue teased my lips, before his teeth grazed my bottom lip. A shiver of anticipation rippled along my spine.

"That is an order I don't want to disobey, *Prince Logan*" I responded with a coy smile.

He slowly rolled onto his back, as his muscles rippled with every move and were hypnotic to watch. I heard a low chuckle escape him before his powerful arms pulled me on top of him. Our chests pressed together, his heart thumping, and his breath heavy against my ear. When his grip loosened, I was able to get into position and fulfill his demand.

My body quivered, as I positioned myself over his face, feeling his hot breath against my most delicate area. Facing his monstrously big shaft, it stood over eight inches. When I tugged at his boxers, it eagerly emerged. I could not wait to see it, under the natural rays of the hazy afternoon sun.

Not only did it look bigger but it felt bigger as my lips stretched around it to accommodate its thickness. His exhalation was hot against my core as I worked his length, matching my rhythm to the thrusts of his fingers inside me. His member stifled my moans as it filled my mouth, taking him to the hilt, and gagging as it reached the back of my throat. As he devoured my flower, my body arched, my breathing heavier as I was edging closer to my climax. *Fuck, I want him,* I thought as I felt his member twitch against my exploring tongue.

"*No!*" Jax roared, his voice shattering my thoughts.

I froze.

Logan's tongue replaced his fingers, penetrating my entrance. He seemed unfazed by his brother's protestation. *Had only I heard his voice?*

"No," came Logan's reply, his words muffled by my heat against his lips. "Ignore him. He will get his turn."

I felt a wash of guilt take over me; it made me feel so cheap and disgusting that I was conflicted between the two. It was predictable that I would be part of similar sexual acts with his brother in due course. For a moment, I felt put off by this situation, but it was soon replaced by the pleasure that was building inside me, inflicted by Logan's persistent and skilled tongue. *Fuck, I am so close.*

I orally pleasured him again, determined to make him ejaculate inside me. Hearing the challenge, he increased his tempo, pressing his thumb against my anus. I froze as I felt his tongue slide up to it.

"Relax," he soothed. "I'll be gentle." He wriggled the tip of his thumb into my virgin entrance, easing the resistance by increasing the tempo of his fingers as they thrashed inside my slit. It was as if I had opened Pandora's box, as wave after wave of pleasure ensued. I craved more, needed more, feeling his determination to give me the best climax I had ever encountered.

As I felt him enter up to his knuckle, an explosion erupted inside of me, causing me to rock against his penetrating fingers as my core pulsated and my rosebud entrance squeezed around his thumb. "Logan!" My voice echoed loudly. "Oh... oh my..." I was out of control as I writhed and bucked with forceful waves circulating inside.

"Cassidy," he groaned, yanking on a fist full of my hair until my mouth released his member. moments before his load pumped from his shaft. Dribbling down his long length. I watched it throb with each spurt, his breathing and groans deepening each time. Transfixed on it, my tongue went to work, licking from the base to the tip, catching the last jets directly in my mouth. Loud moans escaped him as I savored his seed.

Satisfied and exhausted, I rolled off of him, and laid beside him on the blanket. The sun flooded my body with warmth as its rays danced across my bare skin.

I smirked as I stole a glance at him, feeling the butterflies flutter in my stomach as his fingers caressed my bare skin. Instinctively, he pulled me closer to him, encouraging my head to rest on his chest. We stayed that way for a while, recovering from *that*. We breathed slower, eventually matching each other's rhythm.

It had taken a moment for me to realize that the picnic blanket was no longer beneath us. Instead, it was in a tangled mess at our feet. Our bodies now encompassed by the soft tendrils of nature, denting the knee-length grass that was sprinkled with wildflowers. The scent of their floral and earthy fragrance filled my nostrils.

"I never knew eating watermelon could be so much fun!" He smirked, his fingertips tilting my chin up to face him. My face blushed.

"Me neither." When I sat upright, my body protested at the absence of his warm body. My gaze lingered over the lake, absorbing the tranquility of our surroundings. I sighed. "I never want to leave this place."

His eyes twinkled, and then he gently pushed me backward as his lips pinned me into the grass once more. His singular thought penetrated my mind. *I never want to leave you, Cassidy.*

TEN

Logan

The lake was cast in a deep amber that gave it an enchanting, otherworldly glow that sparkled like hundreds of diamonds upon its surface.

Unsurprisingly, after our exertions, we were famished. We devoured the rest of the picnic before reluctantly leaving our sacred spot.

We spoke eagerly of our return tomorrow; my skin tingled in anticipation of what our next encounter might bring. My heart purred with happiness at the thought of being with her, surrounded by the lake's serenity. As we walked hand in hand through Fic, my mind wandered. Before meeting Cassidy, I never knew of its existence. This was a small part of Fic that I had never been allowed to venture when my father was alive. I was glad that the industrial nature of this particular borough had been left untouched. It was beautiful and surreal, just like her.

My head could think of nothing but her. My body responded to hers naturally. Wherever she moved, mine would follow, closing any gaps that may have opened with a kiss. Her hand felt small in comparison to mine, her palm soft as her delicate fingers intertwined with mine. My body thrummed, no longer caring about the tradition of keeping our identities a secret. *If my father could break traditions, who is there to stop me?* All I wanted was to enjoy every moment in her company.

The amount of time we spent together would always be insufficient. We could live forever and a day, and it would not be enough. I wanted to know everything about her, but I also wanted to experience everything Xeyiera had to offer. The thought of having to live without her, sent a cold shiver along my spine as icy tendrils clutched my lungs. *If I had to live without her, my world would be devoid of color and my life would be empty.*

I was drawn to her in ways that reached beyond lust. I craved to see her smile, and this became my focus. If she picked me, I would make her happy in every way possible.

Her foot snagged on a loose stone, and her step faltered. My arm tensed as my other hand reached out to stop her from falling. Her eyes locked onto mine as crimson flooded her cheeks. When she pursed her lips, a small smile flickered on her face while her eyes remained wide in shock.

"I'm sorry *Prince-* I mean, Logan. I'm so clumsy."

I took in her embarrassed expression. Suddenly my mouth was drawn by an unstoppable force, like two magnets, taking us both by surprise. I saw her eyes snap open in panic before they scanned the street, checking to see if anyone had seen us.

"Cassidy, I don't care if someone sees us," I told her, after reluctantly breaking our kiss. "I want them all to know that I am bound to you." The flush in her cheeks grew darker evoking a slight chuckle to escape me as we continued to walk towards her home.

The sun had fallen, and splashes of violet and magenta streaked across the sky. The faint outline of the half-moon was visible. Everything was now washed in a lavender hue. Lanterns along the street lit the path. My muscles relaxed as her body molded into the natural curve of mine. A calm, soothing sensation crept over me like a comforting blanket.

Inner peace was new for me, and I was able to unlock my heart, body, and soul around her. Among nature, our naked bodies side by side, I felt as though I belonged. That precious moment in the tall grass was ours. The secret spot by the lake belonged only to us.

It was only when we neared her house that I sensed my brother's anger. My eyes flitted to Cassidy's face, my mouth opened to tell her, but instantly I snapped it shut. I could not bring myself to awaken her from her contented thoughts. I did not want her to lose the smile that played on her lips nor the spring in her step.

I regretted not telling her, as she stopped dead in her tracks, her eyes open in surprise the moment she spotted Jax standing beside her father in front of her house. Both of them stood at the door, arms crossed with a scowl on their faces.

"Logan, did you know he was here?" she asked in confusion as we stepped into the entrance hall.

I was just about to tell her the truth, when Jax's angry voice interrupted. "Of course, he fucking knew! He knew I wanted to see you, Cassidy, he tried to thwart my plans."

"Jax, I had no knowledge of your plans. I simply wanted to spend some time getting to know Cassidy." I glanced at Cassidy, who I could see had listened to my thoughts. "Your being here was only known to me as we arrived."

"So, wait a minute... *both* of you like Cassidy?" A girl shrieked from the top of the stairs, though several years younger than Cassidy the resemblance was uncanny; same brunette curls and the same slight figure. *"My younger sister, Melody,"* Cassidy confirmed silently as her gaze followed her sister's excited descent to join us. Now, too many bodies cramped the entrance hall. Jax and Cassidy were too close for my liking.

I scowled at him, but then his hand grabbed the collar of my shirt, thrusting me into the closest wall.

"Whoa! Now," her father interjected. "Let's discuss this like adults, shall we?"

Jax let go reluctantly, though the vein in his temple still throbbed in anger.

Her father ushered us into the lounge, insisting that Jax and I sit at either end of the room. Cassidy sat beside her younger sister, and an older lady, who must have been her mother. The three of them looked very similar, yet despite their similarities, Cassidy emitted an elegance and beauty that captivated me. "So... please explain."

Rising to my feet, I found myself once more in charge of speaking. "Hi Mr. Ryvera. I'm Logan." Shaking his hand with a firm handshake, I flashed him a smile. "It seems to be rather *complicated*, Mr. Ryvera. Sir, it appears my brother and I are both bound to your daughter." I told him.

Her father's eyebrows knitted together as his head slightly tilted to one side.

"How is that possible?" her mother asked. "Jax has shared in great detail their special bond and the remarkable night of the Masquerade of Whispers."

"I left out some details." Jax's thought interrupted my mind as a smirk played on his face while Cassidy's cheeks turned a deep shade of scarlet.

"Well, it appears we are both Fated to be her soul mate," I announced to the room, hearing Cassidy heave a sigh of relief that I had changed the subject. "It's incredibly rare, but according to the Elders, not completely unheard of."

"When did you speak to the Elders?" Jax hissed, his eyes narrowed into slits.

"After the party. I needed to alert them of the situation and garner their wisdom on such a matter."

Her father, William, nodded his head slowly. "I always thought it was a myth; that some people were destined to have two soulmates," he muttered, addressing no one in particular. "So, what is going to happen?" He directed his question at me.

"It is for Cassidy to decide." I told him, my eyes darting in her direction. "She has to choose which of us she wants as her mate."

I saw her sister excitedly bounce in her seat and her mother shifted uncomfortably in hers. Cassidy was staring into her hands, resisting the urge to bite her fingernails. I edged closer to Cassidy, reaching for her hand and lacing my fingers into the gaps of hers. "The Elders have agreed to allow Cassidy a month to decide who she wants to claim as her soulmate." I told them, my eyes fixed on her face.

"A month?" her mother asked in shock, her eyes flitting from her daughter to me before lingering on Jax. His body shifted, as his chest puffed up, and as his lips curled into a small smile, she blushed profusely.

"Prince Logan, why is my daughter being given so little time to make such a significant decision?" her father queried.

"The Elders aren't happy about this situation, nor the impact Cassidy's decision will have on the kingdom. They fear our allies will see us as weak, and without a king we are vulnerable to an attack. If I hadn't persuaded Elder Jeremiah to give her a month, she would have one week to make her choice." I responded, keeping my voice calm and my body composed.

It had not been a pretty scene in the Elder's Quarters of Eyre. I shuddered remembering their lewd jokes and their crude statements. It had irked me how crass our supposed founders were, they ruled with an iron fist, but had the mouths of brass sailors.

Cassidy's eyes locked onto mine. I could feel her probing my mind, plucking out the memory and witnessing it for herself. She bit her lip in embarrassment, but the small smile that curled at her lips revealed that she was appreciative of my efforts.

"Thank you, Logan," she whispered as her hand clenched mine.

Jax's eyes narrowed, my hand still laced in Cassidy's hand. My skin still tingled from her warmth, as her grip tightened.

I turned to face Jax, lowering my voice, "Neither of us can consummate our bonds with her until she has publicly announced her chosen mate." I glowered at him, studying his reaction.

Her eyes were cast down to the floor, her embarrassment obvious. *"Must we talk about consummation with my parents?"* Her thoughts flooded my mind, evoking a small grin on my face.

William paced the room, his hands crossed over his chest, deep in thought. "We have to be diplomatic about this. If you are both bound to my daughter, we will need to make arrangements, *fair* arrangements for both of you to see her."

His pacing continued, the staccato beat of his shoes against the wooden floor was the only sound in the room, we were all suspended, waiting for his next words. My pulse throbbed in my ears, the sinking feeling in my gut caused by the thought of not seeing her tomorrow as we had planned.

Her father cleared his throat, abruptly stopping before me. "Logan, do you think it is fair that only one of you should see her each day?" I nodded, watching the corner of his lips curl.

"Jax, do you think it's fair that you and your brother take turns to see her, for example on alternate days?" Jax let William's words sink in, calculating that tomorrow would be his day to see her. With a glint in his eye, he nodded.

"Then that's settled," William announced as if he had just brokered a trade deal. "Some ground rules; Cassidy will not leave this house before eight, and you will both bring her here before eight in the evening... an hour *before* curfew."

Her father's eyes cast over both Jax and I, his smile widening as we both nodded in silent agreement. "Tomorrow, Jax, it will be your turn, considering Logan has been with Cassidy today." he added, much to Jax's delight and my despair.

Cassidy looked between the two of us, her eyes conveying the inner turmoil. I wished there was an easier way, but ultimately, the choice had to be hers. The Elders had said as much, *"The bond will not hold if the decision is made for her. She must choose."*

ELEVEN

Cassidy

Within those four walls of my family home was where the factions between the two Princes first originated. I had not known at the time that it would escalate to catastrophic proportions.

Father, a stickler for formalities and respect, supported Logan. Whereas Mother, the romantic at heart, favored the fantasized story Jax had fed her in our absence. He declared he had known it was love at first sight as soon as he spotted me across the crowded hall at The Masquerade of Whispers.

In those moments, my parents had unwittingly become the first ones to form the two sides of a conflict that would become greater than anyone could have imagined. Melody, however, was torn between them. She wanted me to be happy while she buzzed in the drama's excitement. The four walls of my room closed in around me, tightening around my lungs and squeezing all the air from them. *"You can't be mad at her for being excited, Cass. What fourteen-year-old girl would not be?"*

Flynn's voice filtered into my thoughts. Solemn and matter-of-fact as always. *"This is a BIG deal. It will be spoken about for centuries to come."*

I groaned as I slumped further under the covers in my bed. I needed words of support to lighten the load, not more pressure added to the dead-weight of everyone's expectations on my back.

"Cass, I'm on your team... whoever you decide will be the right choice." He sighed. *"It just can't be made in haste."*

I lay there, staring at the ceiling. Visions of Logan and Jax flitted through my mind. My attraction to them was equal, almost. The extra time spent with Logan today had only made my inner turmoil worse. No matter how hard I tried to fight against the longing for his closeness, images of our encounters would flash through my mind, stirring up the desire for him once more. Every moment I had spent with Logan had been driven by my carnal lust for him, but the attraction to both of them ran deeper than that. The pull of unseen forces in their separate directions felt as though my body and my heart were being torn in half. *What am I going to do?*

"Cass, you have fifteen days to spend with each of them. Use that time wisely."

The sun had barely risen before Jax was at my door, eager to start his day with me. "Jax, it isn't even eight yet." I whispered as I opened my bedroom door. "How did you get in?" His eyes twinkled mischievously. Mother had let him sneak in.

I opened the door, allowing him to enter, suddenly aware that I neglected to do the laundry and tidy my room. He sat on my bed, his eyes exploring every inch of the room. "It's not much," I murmured, fussing about the room, frantically trying to clean it. His eyes clocked the discarded green underwear I had abandoned in a pile of clothes on the floor. My cheeks burned with embarrassment.

"My favorite color is red," he smirked, suddenly on his feet, rifling through my underwear drawer. "Do you have any sexy red lingerie?" My blush deepened, knowing he would soon find out. His fingers pulled out a red lace thong, more elastic string than any other material. "Please tell me you have a matching bra," he gasped, opening a different drawer. "Bingo" his eyes practically popped out of his head. "You shall wear these today." He handed them to me, his lips curled into a sexy smile. "It will be so much fun to get you out of them later." He winked, his body suddenly pressing me against the wall.

I was very aware of how flimsy the material of my nightdress was, how it revealed my bare skin; my legs, arms, and my cleavage all exposed and vulnerable. His thumb grazed over my nipple, feeling the solid peak against the silk fabric. I gasped at the sensation, which only intensified the look of hunger in his eyes. "Cassidy," he murmured, cupping my breast in his hand, using it to hold my body in place against the wall. "You had better keep quiet," he dropped his voice to a whisper. "You don't want your father to catch us."

My core quivered, unsure if that was because of anticipation, as his other hand toyed at the hem of my nightdress. Perhaps it was the thrill of not getting caught. His hand traced the waistline of my knickers. I had not realized I had been holding my breath until he kissed me, his lips were light and playful against mine. I could feel his smirk against my lips while his hand made its way inside my underwear. His fingers teased me, gently stroked the delicate flesh of my mound.

I bit my bottom lip, stifling my moan as he inserted his finger into my entrance while his thumb made small circles against my clit. I felt his thick shaft press against my thigh, and I squealed as he inserted another finger. I could feel my knees grow weak as he worked in a beckoning motion, hard and fast, his thumb frantic against my clit. His mouth planted hot and heavy kisses along the base of my throat, and his teeth grazed the skin. A shot of pleasurable pain shot up through my neck. My eyes opened wide in shock. *"Did you just bite me?"* I mentally asked him, trying to keep my moans as quiet as possible. I was teetering on the brink of climax. His lips planted kisses along my neck, and up to my mouth as his eyes glinted in his amusement.

"I forgot to warn you, I might bite," he responded. A sharp pain penetrated my collarbone as his teeth locked onto my skin. My climax exploded like fireworks; my skin tingled as the sensation overwhelmed me. He brought his fingers up to his lips, sucking my sweet nectar off them, his eyes staring into mine. *"Delicious,"* he moaned silently. *"I can't wait to taste you again."*

As my core trembled in anticipation, my lips sought his. I tasted my tangy sweetness on his tongue. *"I will taste you again but not now,"* he added with a wink. *"You will have to wait until later."*

Still trying to catch my breath, I watched as he made himself comfortable on my bed. "You must have the smallest bedroom I have ever seen." He chuckled. My anger prickled a little, but instead of voicing my thoughts, I went over to my wardrobe, and chose a denim skirt and a plain black t-shirt. "I have never been in Fic before I met you," he said, suddenly standing behind me, his hard member pressing into my buttocks.

It pressed harder against me. The butterflies in my stomach once again active, fluttering their wings uncontrollably. His breath was hot down the back of my neck, as his lips left tantalizing kisses along my jugular. The clothes in my hands fell to the ground.

Turning to face him, my body was desperate for more. Jax's murmur vibrated against my body as his eyes danced with excitement. My hand slid down his chest, feeling the outline of his muscles. "I want to feel those amazing lips of yours..." he groaned, as I lowered myself to my knees in front of his rock-hard manhood.

He did not need to give me any further commands. I unfastened the zipper of his jeans, and pulled them down along with his boxers until they puddled around his ankles. His member stood at attention. I could not help but compare it to Logan's as I took his length into my mouth. Jax's was slightly smaller, but thicker, as it was different in how it stretched the corners of my lips. His hands dug deeper into my hair, using his grasp to control my movements. Thrusting his hips to match my momentum, his lustrous growl grew deeper every time it reached the back of my throat. My tongue danced around him, teasing his tip, feeling it throb beneath it.

I felt him tense, his muscles shudder, and he was quick to pull his member out of my mouth when he reached his climax. Thick sprays of his load released from his shaft, the warm, sticky mess covering my face, trickling down my cheeks and chin. Stunned and speechless, I sat with closed eyes, drenched in spray after spray. "Lick it clean," he demanded, poking my lips with his member. I obeyed; my tongue lapped every last drop.

"Why must you degrade her so, Jax?" Logan's voice cut through the silence. My heart leaped at the sound of his voice. As a flood of guilt washed over me, a small doubt in my mind asked me why I was doing this with Jax.

Jax's arms lifted me to my feet, watching as my tongue licked at the remnants of his load from around my mouth. His finger wiped a small globule of his cum that trickled down my chin and brought it up to his lips. It was erotic seeing him suck it off his own fingertip, enjoying the taste of himself. There was a smirk on his lips. *"I did not think it was degrading. I thought it was sexy as hell,"* Jax murmured, his mouth crashing against mine, erasing any feeling of doubt from my mind. *"You're sexy as Hell,"* he added, his tongue searching for mine.

"Go, have a shower, get dressed... it's almost time!" He gasped, looking at his watch. I gave him a quizzical look as he gathered up my clothes. "Don't forget the red underwear." He winked. As I got into the shower, I could not help but feel lost. Torn between the brothers, my rampant lust for them both was apparent but in different ways. *Both would make very different mates, and lovers.*

As the hot water lashed against my skin; the soap's lavender aroma helped clear my mind. I heard the door open before I could turn around to cover myself. "What are you doing?" I hissed as Jax stood in the middle of the bathroom. My arms crossed across my body, trying to cover myself up as much as possible. "I wanted to see you fully naked, for my eyes only," he murmured.

We were out of the house at exactly, eight-fifteen. We were on horseback, galloping toward the city's gate. "Where are we going?" I asked, holding onto his muscular chest for dear life. Truthfully, I had never been on a horse before and had no idea they still existed. Almost all of the wildlife of Eyre had been driven away by the machines that destroyed their habitat. He shook his head, encouraging the horse to go faster, flying through the castle's huge wrought-iron gates. We stopped among the lush fields, with distant mountains barely visible on the horizon.

"I am taking you to places you have only thought about in your wildest dreams," he shouted, his voice catching on the wind, echoing for miles around us. "Today we are going to Verancas. It's well known for its sandy beaches and lazy tides." He smiled. "My plan is to take you on a journey throughout this entire realm... just the two of us."

My heart leaped; *could I truly be this lucky?* I held onto his waist as our horse slowed, feeling the strange feeling of vertigo overwhelm me. The insides of my thighs felt battered and bruised. "You get used to it." He chuckled, climbing down off the horse, his arms outstretched to help me dismount gracefully. Unfortunately for me, graceful was not my middle name. My foot snagged on the stirrup as I tried to swing my leg around to get free. My hands slipped from the reins, snagging the poor beast's mane, accidentally startling it. Rearing on its hind legs and neighing loudly, it had shaken its body quickly throwing me to the ground.

I looked up at the horse, seeing its magnificent body rise before me, watching as those heavy, thumping hooves lifted from the ground. Higher and higher the horse rose before slowly, and falling back onto the ground. *This is how I'm going to die,* I thought, paralyzed. My eyes fixated on the descending hooves, aware of the imminent danger of being crushed by this majestic creature, helpless to stop it. It was ironic that I would perish the very first time I left Estoria.

In a blur, Jax moved. His arms enveloped me, carrying me with inhuman speed out of the path of the horse's falling hooves. The tremor shook the ground as the horse's front legs connected with the Earth. Jax looked at my face with a teasing smile. "You will need to practice riding a horse, especially *when* you are *my* Queen." He chuckled, his arms tightening around me.

My hands crept behind his neck, pulling me closer to him, kissing him with every ounce of appreciation I could muster. "Thank you, my Prince, for saving my life!" I cooed; my body molded into his.

His eyes sparkled, his thoughts relishing in me calling him by his title as I showed him my gratitude. As his lips pressed against my own, his tongue curled and he whispered, *"You can show me how thankful you are soon."*

TWELVE

Hand outstretched, I whispered incomprehensibly to the beast. In ancient times, humans and animals shared a form of communication. Equus was one of those languages, a way to communicate with their horse companions before going into battle.

"How did you do that?" Cassidy gasped in awe, her eyes flitting between me and the horse.

"My father insisted we learned how to communicate with horses."

At one point in history, it is mentioned that humans had a language for most animals who were used to provide a service. Dogs for herding livestock and horses were used for battle, transport, harvesting crops, and for delivering trading goods to the realms.

Dogs were now wild beasts that roamed the woodland areas along with the wolves and bears. Whereas horses were replaced by technology; automobiles and trains. Their numbers had started declining as humans stopped breeding them.

My father was old-fashioned in his rule. He did not trust automobiles to carry precious cargo or important letters to other parts of the kingdom. My father's disdain stemmed predominately from my mother's death, blaming the slow response because of the busy roads for wasting valuable time, as well as various incidents of letters and parcels arriving too late, if they were even delivered at all. Instead, my father preferred to keep his own stable of horses to deliver any goods and only used a select few trusted messengers to relay his messages.

The stoic nature of my father meant he was unwilling to accept change and as he had done when he was a boy, he ensured all his children learned Equus, and were each given their own horse to feed and look after. As my father always said, *"when technology fails us, we shall always prevail."*

"Take it easy, Sophora." I comforted the horse as I gently caressed her face. "It would be wise for you not to harm the future Queen."

We had traveled a great distance, from Eyre to Verancas. The landscape changed from luscious greenery to a rocky coastline. We had just reached the entrance, at the bottom of Mount Hejha, the largest mountain in the whole of Xeyiera.

Legend has it that the gods formed the mountain to cover the gateway in the fiery underbelly of the world - Hell. It was formed in an attempt to stop evil from escaping and to seal in the tormented souls of the condemned. Yet, at the very peak of the mountain the Heavens sat. Covered by clouds, it remained unseen, a legend in its own right.

Only a handful of people have attempted to climb Mount Hejha and explore its caves, to prove or disprove this legend, though none had lived to tell of their findings. Cassidy was staring up at the mountain, her face a picture of wonder. Her eyes animated in her delight.

"Wow!" had been the only word she had mustered as her eyes swept across its rocky surface. For a few moments, I allowed her to admire the mountain, before distracting her with a kiss.

"There are many more delights to behold." I informed her, taking her hand in one of mine, while the other held Sophora's reigns, guiding them both along the rocky coastal path that bordered the base of the mountain.

By late morning, we had arrived at the sandy beach across the mountain. Verancas was tucked away at one of the edges of the world. A small Kingdom, but one that held great importance. It provided only one important component Eyre used for the creation of its infamous industrial trades: Thyram. The mineral was only found here where it had been naturally formed within its sandy beaches. The people of Verancas relied on our ever-growing demand for this mineral, sifted by hand.

It had made their hierarchy rich beyond their wildest dream. The discovery of its uses in technology was helpful. Our reputation for crafting items withstood the test of time.

Those at the bottom of the pecking order sieved the coast's beaches for the mineral. Traders reaped the rewards. They were paid a pittance for their hard work, yet the material itself was sold for eye-watering sums. I left the procurement negotiation to Logan. We were not here for business; we were here for pleasure.

As we entered the sleepy town of Verx, that bordered the first beach, it was easy to discern it abandoned. A ghost town. In the shadow of Mount Hejha, the inhabitants found solace within the walls, especially in Kopli, the central hub of all activities.

Tethering Sophora to the visitors' stable, I filled her bowl of water and retrieved a bundle of hay from the trough. "Feed her," I gestured to Cassidy. "While I go and find a friend, Alyiah." She looked hesitant, scared. Pulling a sugar cube out of my pocket, I offered it to her. "Sophora's favorite." I winked, before leaving her.

I waltzed through the grounds of the stables, finally reaching the wooden hut she called home. When I approached it, the door was ajar. Peering through the crack, I saw Alyiah's tanned slender body, naked, sprawled on the floor while another woman, one I did not recognize, greedily devoured her heat. My shaft twitched at the sight. Only then did the soft moans of her pleasure filter through to my eardrums.

"What are you – *oh!*" I hadn't heard Cassidy approach and I had been unsure how long I had been standing there watching them. Cassidy's eyes briefly left the scene, dropping to my groin. My member held firm in my hand outside my pants. It was so instinctive to stroke my member as I watched them. I had almost forgotten about her company.

"Isn't this wrong?" she whispered, her hand replacing mine, her eyes snapping back to them, the two women in the throes of passion. Her voice was thick, clogging her throat.

"Not here." I moaned as her hand gripped my shaft tighter, pumping it harder each time. "Here, love is love. Regardless of gender." I added, my voice purring as I spoke. "Pleasure is pleasure."

Alyiah cried out as her orgasm gripped her. We watched in silence as her body trembled. Her perky nipples tilted in the air like two mountain peaks. As I recalled the feel of Alyiah's soft skin beneath my lips, I remembered her taste. A trip here was never complete without seeing Ayliah.

Cassidy's anger prickled beside me. Her hand stilled on my shaft. She stopped watching the women who were still pleasuring each other, their moans becoming a gentle murmur. Instead, her narrowed eyes were set on my face, her lips pursed into a taut line.

"Jealousy is cute on you," I whispered, kissing her forehead. "But there is no need to be jealous of Ayliah. She was only ever a bit of no-strings fun, she is not my mate, and she is definitely not *you*." I purred, pulling her face closer to mine.

"I brought you here, not to make you jealous, but to experience this place. For the views more so than for pleasure. Though, I am not complaining." I soothed, planting hot and impatient kisses along her nape.

"Would you like to join them?" I asked her, raising my eyebrow. Her pulse raced under my touch, revealing that she was aroused by my suggestion. My hand slid down to her denim skirt, feeling her skimpy lace underwear beneath my fingertips, recalling how those red undergarments looked. My member throbbed impatiently.

"Can we?" she murmured, her head rolling backwards, her pants quickening as her slit devoured my fingers.

With a creak, the door opened, and there stood Alyiah, completely naked, as her eyes locked on us.

"Come in," she beckoned. Cassidy stood frozen; cheeks flushed with embarrassment for getting caught observing them.

"You Estorians do love to watch," she giggled, holding the door open for our entrance. Her blush deepened, torn between shame for being discovered and the reluctance to release my member from her grasp.

"Oh darling, we possess items far greater than fingers," Ayliah whispered, as Cassidy hesitantly passed her and stepped into the wooden lodge. "We have *toys* that are much *larger* too," she added.

THIRTEEN

Cassidy

My face burned with embarrassment, flames licking from within, leaving me unsure where to gaze. His shaft remained firm in my grip, and his fingers still nestled between my legs, as a nude woman opened the door. Her face was unfazed, as if seeing us caught pleasuring ourselves, spying on their intimate act, was a normal occurrence.

My anger still seethed at him; my jealousy derived from my inexperience and their intimate past Jax thought so fondly of. I had been waiting for my mate. He already has experience with other women. Ayliah being one of them.

"A man has needs," his voice pleaded inside my mind for my understanding as jealousy coursed through me. *"If I had met you sooner, I would not have needed her."*

As I entered the wooden hut, the other woman's eyes were trained on us from the couch, her hand absentmindedly toyed with her heat. My cheeks burned in my shame. Their illicit actions had turned me on, and had made me act so carelessly.

My steps were tentative, my core tingled and excitement thrummed through my body. The thought of them using forbidden toys on me, made my head spin.

The Elders had prohibited the use of "phallic objects" in their intention to preserve the sacred act of consummating. It was their belief that such items encouraged 'false bonds' between the same genders that disrespected the values and beliefs upheld in the Rules of Conduct.

In the depths of my most profound desires, I had never imagined using such a tool. Alyiah smirked, clearly sensing the shock I felt, mixed with fear and insatiable desire.

Beside me, Jax exuded a bemused aura, exhibiting his amusement at my unease. My heart throbbed in my ears, finding myself in this unfamiliar territory. I was a lamb that had been led to the lion's den.

Silently, the two women began unveiling me. His eyes meticulously observed their every gesture, relishing each unfolding moment as they gracefully removed each garment, exposing my nakedness to them all. The woman purred as her fingers traced over my skin. "I am Eleanor, and I must say, you are gorgeous."

Before I could respond or feel any embarrassment, her lips locked onto mine. Ayliah sank to her knees in front of me, her face suddenly at my heat. Her hot breath and wild tongue movements intensified the sensations between my legs.

Taken by surprise, I let out a squeal, prompting them to continue with smirks stretched across their faces. Out of the corner of my eye, I saw Jax slowly stroking his member. He licked his lips as he enjoyed the sight of Ayliah's tongue greedily lapping at my slit.

I groaned against Eleanor's lips as Aliyah's tongue darted in and out of my entrance. My knees were weak, but Eleanor's strong hands on my breasts gave me the strength to remain standing upright. "Do it," Jax ordered. His eyes narrowed. "Show her."

Ayliah opened a small wooden crate to the side of her, an assortment of brightly colored, phallic-looking objects lay in the box. My eyes widened in shock. Ayliah retrieved a small, smooth red one, taking it in her mouth. The loud whir of vibrations ricocheted off her teeth, her cheeks shaking, her smile growing at the hunger in Jax's eyes.

My jealousy prickled once more, the intimate history between them tangible as she took the item into her mouth as she would have his shaft. Within an instant, the vibrations flooded my core as she held the item against my clit. Her tongue returned to my entrance. "I think you're ready," she purred, as she slid the tip into me.

I took a sharp intake of breath, as the head of it stretched my opening. Jax moaned, his eyes focused on the toy. My core pulsated as she pushed it deeper. A flood of panic spread through me as my walls clenched around it. The pain of the stretch made me refuse to let it go any deeper. "Jax, I can't..." I whispered, trying to back out of the girl's grip,

"Of course you can," he purred, stepping forward. He took it from Ayliah, pressing the vibrating item against my resistance, his other hand frantic against my nub. It entered bit by bit until my inner walls were fully stretched. I cried out. His hand stilled as he waited for the pain to subside. The item thrummed deep inside me, inflicting my nectar to flow between my legs. Realizing this he started vigorously pumping it in and out of me, taking advantage of the now slick entrance.

My orgasm hit me like a punch to the stomach, ripping the air out of my lungs. My thoughts shattered; my vocal cords rendered useless. A fire ripped through my body as my core clutched at the object. "Don't you wish that was me?" He moaned, as his breathing grew heavy.

Eleanor laid on the floor, her mouth devoured Ayliah's heat, while Alyiah's mouth enveloped Jax's manhood. I clenched my fist, as I tried to ignore my jealousy, but I could not take my eyes off her mouth as it worked his shaft expertly. He could sense my unease, and gave me his undivided attention.

The phallic object thrust deeper into my core, as his hot breath whispered in my ear, "She means nothing. She's just a means for my pleasure. I want you." His eyes darkened, as his lips brushed against mine. "I wish it was me deep inside you," he groaned.

Ayliah's cry of pleasure gurgled in her throat as Jax shot his load, his lips crashing against mine, his hand working the phallic object in and out of me furiously. My knees buckled and my muscles clenched as my climax tore through my body. A scream involuntarily escaped my lips as I trembled in its aftermath. I clutched onto Jax for support, a smirk plastered across his face. "I'll be next," he whispered. "And it will be *much* better than that."

With a quick flick of his wrist, he threw the object to the floor. The vibrations suddenly stopped. He did not care. I was pushed back onto the couch, my legs splayed in the air, while his mouth lapped up my nectar. So sensitive was my core that he inflicted another orgasm within a minute. His eyes glanced into mine. "Look at them," he groaned. Obeying his command, my eyes flew to them. Eleanor had a contraption strapped to her, making her look as if she had male genitalia.

The shaft was transparent and veiny, showing one end inserted into her heat, while the tip on the outside teased Ayliah's. My lust and my desire grew as my inhibitions diminished. *I want to feel that.* His eyes snapped up to mine, his mouth suctioning over my clit. "Eleanor, why don't you take Cassidy first?" He winked.

There was no stopping her. Her eyes narrowed in determination as she thrust her hips against mine, splaying my legs wider in the air, her hands wrapped around my ankles. Jax stood over me, his hard shaft pushing open my mouth once more. It pulsated against my tongue, his groan louder as it slid to the back of my gagging throat.

The wet, sloshing sound of the object pounding into me rang in my ears, accompanying his groans. It was not long until my body gave out, bucking and writhing against the object, as my throat swallowed the last of his seed. My persistent eye-contact pleased him even as I struggled to breathe.

Panting, I held my hands up in surrender, my heat throbbing painfully as Eleanor retreated, turning her attention to Ayliah who had been patiently toying with herself with another phallic object. The one that stretched her hole was bigger than anything humanly possible. My eyes could not make sense that something that big could ever fit in there.

Jax's soft chuckle snapped me back to reality, his member now fastened back into his pants. "Let's leave them to it," he whispered. "Let me show you the real reason I brought you here." Eleanor and Ayliah were too engrossed in their ecstasy to notice we were leaving.

I felt Logan inside my mind, his lust gripped my every thought. Logan wanted me, despite his anger at the situation Jax had placed me in.

"Cassidy, you should not have done that," Logan panted. I felt my body shudder with his body. Our telepathic connection was getting stronger, I could feel what he was feeling. *Did he feel what I had been feeling too?*

For a split second, I saw out of Logan's eyes, that his pulsating member bore streaks of his white, creamy seed that had ruptured over his hand.

"Did you just... were you watching us...?" I asked, bewildered, and aroused.

Logan cut the connection without another word, his embarrassment at being caught partaking in voyeurism. I looked at Jax, his face blank and expressionless.

"It appears he enjoyed seeing you get fucked by her more than he would care to admit," he muttered. *How long has Jax known that Logan is watching us?*

Just then Jax scooped me up in his arms, and wrapped my legs around his waist, pinning me against the outside of Ayliah's house. "I, on the other-hand, will openly admit that was the hottest thing I had ever seen." His voice purred as his lips flitted over my neck.

"If you choose me, situations like that can happen more often, as we travel from Kingdom to Kingdom." Jax continued as his mouth planted hot, impatient kisses along my collarbone. "I will also lift the ban on *toys.*" His eyes glinted mischievously.

My core moistened at the thought of it. *Do I want to experience more of that? Or would I just want to keep Jax all to myself?*

The wind whipped through my hair, sending tendrils scattered about my head in a frenzy. I could taste the ocean, the air heavy with salt, as we stood at the water's edge. The waves swept delicately over our feet, dragging the gritty sand over them as they were sucked back out to sea. The ocean tide crashed and angrily tumbled. Their roars of fury were deceiving as they filled our ears with their aggression. A stark contrast to the gentle trickle that washed over our feet, turning into nothing more than a feeble hiss, as the sand fizzed beneath the current.

I wiggled my toes, feeling the sand mold to my footprint, mesmerized by the tranquility of the moment. Just being and breathing. Being here with Jax was surreal as I watched the sun creep across the horizon, seeing it reflect on the shoreline at the end of the Earth.

"I'm scared, Cassidy," he admitted, picking up a pebble from beside his foot. "This bond, it's real, you know." He flicked his wrist, releasing the tiny rock at just the right time to make it skip across the water.

"I know." I exhaled, picking up my pebble, trying to recreate the skipping stone. Mine, however, just plopped straight into the waves with a loud splash. It was a catastrophic failure.

"Here, let me show you," he said as he placed the pebble in my hand, positioning my fingers so that the pebble was resting on my curled middle finger, my thumb holding it in place.

"You use this finger," he said, gently touching my forefinger. "To guide the rock where you want it to go. If you keep your wrist flat and flick it like this, it will skim the water. Go on, you try."

He stood close to me, his breath warm on the back of my neck. I tasted the salt that lingered in the crisp sea breeze. The sensation of the two temperatures sent a shiver along my spine. After counting to three, I released the rock. This time, it bounded twice before succumbing to the waves.

"I did it!" I cheered, turning around to face him. My arms wrapped around his neck in my elation. "Let's do it again!" I said. "Let's keep doing it until mine beats yours!" His chuckle resonated through his body, throaty and deep, before falling into a long silence. Our foreheads touched as we stared into each other's eyes.

"It's daunting to know that one of us will never have another soul mate... that one of us will have to live without *you.*" The intensity of Jax's gaze sent a shiver along my spine.

"I'm scared too, Jax. I'm scared that I will make the wrong choice."

"That is what I am afraid of, too," he murmured, breaking away from me to pick up a slightly bigger pebble and skimming it elegantly across the waves.

Silence blanketed us for a few moments, as we both watched the sun glimmering on the soft ripples of the waves. I quickly glanced over at him. His eyes were glazed over, his eyes cast out to the open ocean, completely lost by his thoughts, and consumed by the inner turmoil of his feelings,

Anger and jealousy thrashed through him as he plucked at memories of me and Logan together, lamenting on the connection I also held with his brother. One question swirled in his mind; *when will she make up her fucking mind? Why the fuck hasn't she chosen me yet?*

I wanted to make him happy by answering his thoughts, to tell him what he wanted to hear - that I had made my decision. But I could not lie to him. *I refuse to lie to him.* Jax's head suddenly whipped around to face me. His eyes lit up, and his face softened.

"You're beautiful, Cassidy," he murmured. "Inside and out." His face drew closer to mine, and our noses were touching. "I've never been allowed to have anything as beautiful before," he whispered, his lips grazing over mine. "Logan always got the new shiny things. Mine were his cast-offs, tarnished and ruined."

I felt myself fall deeper into his embrace; my lips fluttered against his. "Jax, I don't know what the future holds," I murmured, feeling my insides succumb to the warmth of his gaze. "Let's just enjoy the here and now."

I heard him sigh. His aura prickled angrily; his hands balled into fists at his side. "But *you do*, Cassidy." His eyes pierced mine, penetrating my thoughts in the hope of finding the answer he so desperately wanted. He turned his head away from me, his eyes cast out once more to the open ocean. My gaze followed his, as I leant my head against his cheek.

The sun glowed a dark orange, as streaks of scarlet slashed across the azure blue of the sky, casting us and everything beneath it in an ethereal pink hue.

His gaze was intense as his eyes locked onto mine "Cassidy, you have the power to choose what *our* future holds."

FOURTEEN

Logan

It has been a long time since the peace inside Eyre had been disrupted. Yet in the space of a week, the kingdom has divided itself in two, and now there was another problem that I needed to deal with; twenty-foot tall, bloody-thirsty, and highly dangerous uninvited visitors.

Trolls had always been a part of Xeyiera's world; they were in legends and mythical stories, and they still exist today. Throughout time, they had lived peacefully in their parts of the world, in treacherous mountains and perilous plains, swamplands and bogs. For as long as I have lived there had not been a singular troll sighting anywhere near Eyre, let alone an attack. Yet, according to this letter signed by Chief Ivan of Svaalgard, there were two attacks in his kingdom alone, this past week.

I tried to concentrate on the map on the wall, the small dots showing where the attacks had taken place, but all I could think about was Cassidy spending the day with *Jax.*

I did not want to share her, especially not with him, but I had no choice. I was honorable with my word, and I had agreed to the terms with her father. *But just because I had agreed does not mean that I am happy about it.*

I needed to gather as much information on the trolls; I have never dealt with these creatures before. It was impossible to figure out a plan, a strategy. *They must have a leader, perhaps I should appeal to them, to get the answers I need-*

My heart rate quickened, and my thick shaft throbbed against the zipper of my pants. *What the fuck?*

My vision blurred, as I saw shapes and colors, and then, I heard the sound of Cassidy's moaning. These were similar to the moans she had made with me, only more intense.

Furrowing my brow the vision became clearer; I was no longer looking at the map inside my father's study. Instead, I was watching a taboo scene through Cassidy's eyes. Two olive skinned beauties were ravaging her body, one rolling Cassidy's nipples in slow tantalizing circles, while the other greedily lapped at her quivering core.

The strangest part was that I could *feel* everything: Cassidy's lust, her desire to be pushed over the edge of her climax, her want for *more*. My hand absentmindedly wrapped around my shaft, watching the scene unfold, as illicit toys were brought into play. Its vibration thrummed through me, enjoying the pleasure buzz as it rippled through my body.

I scowled in frustration, knowing I had no right to eavesdrop on their day together, but the suddenness of our connection had consumed me. There was nothing I could do except watch what was happening as I stroked my engorged member, beating it as hard and as fast as I could. I enjoyed it even more because I could *feel* Cassidy's orgasms. She developed an ever-increasing hunger for more, keeping me hooked, wanting to watch and experience it all. My load exploded more forcefully than I had ever experienced the moment she succumbed to her final climax.

I was left dazed, too stunned to move. Panting heavy, the white, and sticky mess was all over my hand, trickling down my shaft. The moment I heard Cassidy's voice in my head, I knew I had been caught watching them. Shame and embarrassment instantly flooded into me. Hearing her gasp as she too saw the proof all over my groin demonstrating how their tryst affected me.

All I was capable of doing was blocking them out as the shame and embarrassment of being caught, when Cassidy had sensed me watching her, consumed me.

The room was spinning, and I felt lightheaded as I tried to awkwardly clean myself up. When I was sliding my shaft back into my pants, the oak door of the study burst open.

Demi's eyes narrowed at me suspiciously, her eyes dropping to my hands on my crotch and then the crumpled tissues in the trash. I tried to steady my breath, to ignore the awkwardness in this moment, grateful she had not walked in a moment sooner.

"Have you heard about the trolls?" she asked, slamming down another letter on the desk. "Logan, what are you going to do about it?"

Her long blonde hair tumbled past her shoulders, stopping just above her hips. It shimmered under the sunlight, making it appear translucent. It appeared almost thin and translucent in comparison to the deep purple velvet dress she was wearing. She appeared ethereal, not like Jax's twin nor my younger sister. In fact, she looked more like a mythical witch from pages of our childhood tales.

"Logan- This letter, it's from Vrek, their king wants action. Trolls have been spotted heading out in different directions across the whole of Xeyiera." A look of genuine panic was etched into her face. "Something needs to be done - *you* need to do something!"

"Demi, what am I supposed to do?"

She shrugged, folding her arms across her chest. "They are heading here, Logan, they could be heading toward Cassidy and Jax too."

My brows furrowed. "How do you know? Where the *fuck* are they Demi?" I could not gain a telepathic link with her; she had guarded her mind from me since the age of six, when I had found out that it had been her and Jax breaking into the pantry, eating all of the chocolate and sweets, even though I had been the one who was getting blamed. She had never forgiven me for exposing them; pretty petty considering that was nearly twenty years ago.

"Demi, where the *fuck* did Jax take Cassidy? She could be in danger." My anger flared, and streaks of red obscured my vision as I stared at her uncompassionate face. I changed tack, "Well, if Jax gets hurt, there will be no opposition to me taking the throne."

"Argghhhh..." Demi glowered, "Fine. Verancas... that's where Jax took Cassidy."

My eyes shot to the map, snatching the letter from beneath her hands, adding additional pins to the other confirmed sightings. I heard Demi's low whistle in the background. "That's a lot of red dots." Her tone seemed somewhat amused. "Something has really riled them up - it is not a case of a sole wanderer, there are too many of them. *This is an invasion.*"

I frowned at her and then back at the map. *Shit.*

"So, what's your plan?" she asked, her boots tapping incessantly against the wooden floor. "The longer you *don't* do something... the worse it looks on *you.* How could the kingdom trust you to protect them as the next king if you sit here and do nothing?"

Why did I listen to Demi? I asked myself, as I stalked along the outskirts of Eyre, distanced from the Royal Guard. Through the thick and dense woodlands along the way, I seemed to have become separated from my security detail. Instead, the odds were no longer in my favor; the plan was to have eight men in tow, reinforcements in case the trolls did not want to cooperate peacefully, but now there was just me.

I gulped as I took in their ominous figures as they towered over the ancient trees, their rough-skin resembling the mountainous terrains in which they lived. They were huge walking, talking boulders, with moss on their backs, and brown eyes glaring at me.

"What do you want, human?" The deep, dulcet tone of the troll boomed, causing the leaves to rustle under his breath.

"Why are you here?" I asked, trying to remain calm despite the quiver in my voice.

"Look, Prince," his eyes narrowed as his body stooped low toward me. "We are free to roam where we like."

"Who told you such nonsense?" I shouted, refusing to cower from him.

"We do not need to be told anything!" The other troll thundered, two of them standing before me. Trolls were rumored to be stupid, obviously this was not the case with these. They circled me. Their vast size made them irrefutable victors, and if a fight were to happen, I could not take them out on my own. I glanced from one to the other, watching over my shoulders, hoping that by a miracle, the guards would appear at any moment.

"Vruut, our leader." The one closest troll said to me. "I'm Keib, Vruut's second in command." His arm gestured to the other troll. "He is Rabb, my brother."

I frowned at him, as he held up his hand to silence Rabb who had opened his mouth to speak. "Why would Vruut say that? My father, the King, he said there was a treaty-"

"Vruut has grown tired of our *habitat*. He was offered a proposition and he took it." Keib said with a smirk, "In fact, we were on our way to get *you*. You were the bargaining chip that would seal Vruut's deal."

I had no time to register the shock of his words as Rabb charged in my direction, determination, and fury in his eyes. On his approach, I quickly sidestepped him and ducked between his legs.

He let out a loud growl in frustration. Keib started thumping its giant wooden club against the ground. The length of it matched those of nearby trees, making the earth tremor beneath my feet.

Birds squawked as they deserted their nests in the trees. I needed to find out more about this *proposition*, and where I could find Vruut. I figured the best way would be to hide and wait for my guard to arrive so that they would grow tired of searching. But Keib was raking the ground with his club, leveling trees, and shrubbery in his determination to find me.

I danced and weaved around the fallen forest as adrenaline pumped through my veins, pushing me to keep moving. Looking over my shoulder I saw that their size made it difficult to meet my agility, unable to pivot as quickly or run fast enough. Their long legs allowed them to effortlessly stride over the toppled trees, while I had no choice but to grapple over the ones I could not navigate around.

Rabb was hot on my heels, but had somehow lost his footing, falling beside me as if in slow motion, causing a crater as he hit the ground. Its impact sent out shockwaves across the land, and shuddered through every bone in my body, causing me to fall to the ground.

Out of the corner of my eye, I saw Keib trying to flank me, swinging his club once more, ignoring his brother lying unconscious before me. "Your father was a good man, a righteous King..." the troll growled, his footsteps stomping slowly toward me. "You are a coward... refusing to stand and fight me like a man..."

He lunged, and his hand caught me, squeezing me in his palm. The strength of his unyielding grip crushed my arms to my sides and I could feel every bone in my body verging on the brink of snapping. I struggled to breathe. All I could think of was Cassidy's face.

"What...do... you... want?" I wheezed, unable to unsheathe the sword at my hip. "I... did not...come...to...fight...."

Rabb had scrambled to his feet, his body oozing black tar-like blood as branches impaled his torso. "We want blood," he growled, wincing as he tried to remove one sharp branch from his skin. Keib shook his head, baring his teeth, and hissed as he spoke, "No...Rabb, we are doing this so we can be free."

I was suddenly falling, unable to grab onto anything to stop myself. I hit the ground hard, the air knocked from my lungs, as the entire right side of my body exploded in agony, but my eyes stayed transfixed on the two trolls, who seemed to have temporarily forgotten about me and instead were focused on one another. Their faces revealed their confusion as they bickered.

I tried to sneak away, dragging myself to my feet. An intense pain shot through my right arm as I tried to remove the sword from its sheath at my side, my fingers reluctant to respond. *Shit.*

Warm blood streamed from a gash on my forehead. I kept my eyes on the trolls as I slunk into the shadows, hoping to put some distance between us. *Is there no other option than to kill them?*

Their voices boomed through the air as their fists pushed one another. Each troll was determined to land a more catastrophic blow than the last. The ground quaked as their feet stomped, their roars echoing loudly, drowning out all other sounds.

For several moments, I stood silently watching them. The club cracked against the side of Raab's skull, his eyes widened in shock before narrowing into slits, a growl resonated from his chest as blood oozed from the wound. He tried to take a step toward Keib before falling to the ground like a dead weight. The ground quaked once more, causing the branches that were hiding me to fall.

Keib's eyes locked onto me, snarling in anger as he charged. Crimson rivulets flowed from every wound on his body, though he showed little affliction for his injuries. His eyes were bloodshot red, and his veins protruded from its neck. His knuckles dragged along the dusty ground as he stomped in my direction.

My pulse quickened, violently pounding in my ears with every step closer he got. I willed my arm to grasp the sword, ignoring the pain that shot through my body as I thrust it toward him. It pierced Keib's flesh but it was not a fatal wound. His hand threw me several feet through the air until my spine crashed into a trunk of a nearby tree.

I throbbed in pain. Determined not to die, adrenaline surged as I longed to see Cassidy once more. I would not let anything, not even a troll, stop me from seeing her again.

"I never understood why humans would try to fight us." Keib's steps were sluggish as he circled me, growing weaker. It gave me the opportunity to scramble to my feet, my sword still clutched in my hand. "You humans are too weak." He growled.

There was a movement behind him, a shadow that darted between the trees. I could not make out who or what it was, but it jumped onto Keib's back. Two human-like hands covered the troll's eyes, and their fingers gouged at the sockets.

The troll crumpled to its knees; cries of pain filled the air. *"Now!"* came a voice in my mind. My eyes snapped to the figure, his floppy brown hair streaked with blood, only holding onto the troll's thighs.

Looking at the target, I launched myself toward it, blade forward, confident in my skill to cause the intended damage. Adrenaline pulsed through my body, temporarily overriding the pain as I swung the sword with both hands on the hilt. A roar escaped me as the sword slashed through the air.

I heard the slickness of flesh when it tore beneath my sword's razor-sharp blade. A spray of hot scarlet covered me as it sliced through the troll's neck, severing it completely. Its head tumbled in the same direction as my blade, while his body fell to the other side.

Struggling for breath, I stumbled toward the headless corpse. A human hand protruded from underneath its body, limp and lifeless.

Cassidy's voice rang in my ears, her agony piercing my heart as I tried to roll the troll's corpse off this unknown savior. Digging my heels into the ground, using the very last of my energy, I pushed back against the headless body, until it shifted, exposing the fearless warrior whose distraction had saved me. My blood ran cold as my eyes swept over his lifeless form. My heart stopped.

Cassidy's voice took the last of the air from my lungs. *"Flynn!"*

FIFTEEN

My stomach churned and bile rose in the back of my throat. *How could things go so wrong on such a good day?*

Seeing Flynn lying unconscious through Logan's eyes made my blood run cold. I had been selfish, blocking my mind from distractions so that Jax and I could revel in each other's pleasure in Verancas. *If we were still in Eyre, I could have gotten to him. I could have healed him.*

Disgust filled me. While I had been engulfed in orgasms, Logan had been fighting for his life.

"Is he breathing?" I asked Logan telepathically, ignoring the resonating anguish in his lingering thoughts; I heard and felt them. Logan remained focused so he could see me once more.

Every muscle in my body felt numb as I studied Flynn through Logan's eyes. There was a peaceful expression on Flynn's face as if he were sleeping. *"Please don't say he is dead!"*

Logan pressed his fingers against Flynn's neck, as his sigh of relief temporarily soothed me. *"What the fuck happened?"* I asked Logan, seeing the bloody scene before him. Two trolls were slumped on the ground, one of which was decapitated, its severed head lay in a pool of dark scarlet blood.

Jax scooped me up onto Sophora's back, encouraging me to wrap my arms tightly around him before digging his heels into her sides. Her hooves battered against the grasslands, tearing up chunks of the earth in her urgent strides. *"Why are there trolls in Eyre?"* I asked, my voice desperate for Logan to respond. *"Why did they attack you?"*

Logan remained silent for a few moments. *"The trolls want freedom from their lands."* Logan sighed. He scooped up Flynn's lifeless body, his arms and legs dangling as a ragdoll.

Logan started to walk back to the kingdom, his steps faltered and he swayed unsteadily on his feet, his voice came in short pants in his struggle to walk through his own pain. *"Their leader Vruut was offered a proposal, that stated they wanted me to die in order for them to be free."* An involuntary gasp escaped me, and my nails dug into Jax's skin. He tensed beneath my fingertips.

"Who would make such an offer to the trolls?" My question was met with a stony silence, creating a tension so palpable it could be cut with a knife.

It felt as if it had taken forever to get to Logan and Flynn, meeting them along the dusty road. Logan fell to his knees, his body battered, his cuts bleeding and staining the remnants of his tattered clothes, as he cradled Flynn like a baby.

I crashed down onto the grounds beside them. My left hand brushed over Flynn's body feeling for his wounds while my right hand tried to feel a pulse against his neck. It grew weaker by the second.

A sob escaped me as I summoned my ability to heal him. A white light emanated from my palms, as I held them on Flynn's chest, watching as it was absorbed by his flesh, blazing as it coursed through every vein and artery inside his body, lighting up their path like a tangle of fluorescent wires. I could feel myself growing weaker as the path of the light spread throughout his body until finally ending up behind his eyes. They flickered momentarily.

My relief came out as another sob, as he slowly blinked, his eyes trying to adjust to see my face looming over him. My body collapsed against him, embracing him in a fierce hug, as my sobs trembled through my body.

"Cass?" he groaned; his voice raspy. "Trolls...."

I put my finger to his lips, hushing him. "Don't try to speak" I reassured, brushing his hair out of his face. "Relax." I soothed, holding his hand in mine. "Let me finish healing you." My heart rate slowed, synchronizing with Flynn's as the last of my strength left my body; willing it to repair the fractures, and stitch up any internal ruptures and bleeds caused by his body being crushed under the weight of the troll's corpse.

I heard the tense exchange between the brothers, but I was too focused on using my healing power to help Flynn.

Logan's words were faint, but there was no denying his anger. "Jax, are you trying to kill me?"

The nagging doubt that lingered in my mind, had also gnawed at my insides causing a wave of nausea to envelope me. "Jax, did you know about this?" My voice cracked, eyes narrowing at him as he dropped to his knees by my side. Resting his head on my shoulder, his guilt flooded my mind.

"I-I did not know, n-not," he exhaled deeply. "I just—"

"He wanted to keep me busy. So that he could have your undivided attention." Logan snapped.

"Is this true?" I asked Jax, fearing the answer he would give.

"I asked Demi to distract Logan, yes. But I did not know-" Jax's jaw clenched as he got to his feet and squared up against his brother. It was the first time I had seen them stand next to each other. Jax was half a head shorter than Logan, his physique not as broad or muscular. His youth made him hot-headed, short-tempered, and rash in his decision making.

"You still managed to wriggle in, though, didn't you?" Jax fumed; his hands balled into fists. "You still had to get yourself involved *somehow*." Jax's fist swung through the air, catching Logan by surprise. A sickening crunch ricocheted as his fist connected with Logan's jaw. Instinctively Logan grabbed the Jax by the scruff of the collar, lifting him a few feet in the air in retaliation.

"Stop!" I yelled, unable to leave Flynn, the process of his healing still incomplete. My energy source was depleting faster than expected because my focus was split between the scenes unfolding before me. "Please stop." I sobbed.

Logan let go of Jax, staggering backward, but Jax refused to back down, his smirk revealing his confidence against the already weakened Logan. The injuries Logan had sustained against the trolls meant he would not be as strong as he would normally be.

Logan sighed as he clutched at his right side of his body. "Just admit it Jax, you did not care to know her plans... you were too hellbent on trying to defile and disrespect Cassidy." He muttered, wincing as he tried to wipe the blood that started oozing from his split lip.

I tried to reach them in my mind, but the inky black hue that had been slowly creeping around the edges of my vision was now smothering everything and blinding my view of them all.

Their voices grew faint, their words nothing but a thrum as I felt myself falling through the darkness that overcame me. Before long I was not aware of anything, but the silence of the black abyss I had fallen into.

I was suspended on clouds, my body sinking into their softness, feeling cozy and snug. I drifted through a restless slumber; images of Flynn's broken body flashed through my mind, accompanied by the conflicting scenes of being with Jax, while Logan fought with every inch of his life. A searing pain flashed through my right temple. My stomach churned in the realization that I did not deserve Logan. I was too selfish for someone as kind-hearted and loyal as him.

"Cassidy..."

I tried desperately to open my eyes, to see the person whose voice it belonged to, hoping it was Logan by my side. While I may not have deserved his love, I *wanted* it. I needed it more than anything I had ever needed before.

"You deserve the world," the husky voice whispered. "You deserve more than what I could ever give you..." I felt his lips flutter over the back of my right hand, stirring me into consciousness.

"W-where am I?" I croaked, my eyes blinking around the room, taking in the regal patterns that adorned the walls, swirls of deep burgundy and gold. Dark wooden panels accompanied it, which matched with the wood furnishings, including the giant four-post bed frame I was currently laid in. It was the soft mattress that molded to my body, giving the impression that I was floating weightlessly on the fluffy clouds in the sky.

The bed swallowed my hand as I tried to sit up, a pair of hands caught me before I toppled to the side, and he helped hoist me to sit upright.

"How are you feeling?" the voice asked, his hands encompassing mine. His blue eyes staring at me, deep with worry. I could not disguise my disappointment in my thoughts, causing a flicker of hurt to flash across his face. It was not Logan by my side offering me comfort.

"Jax?" I murmured, my free hand reaching out to his face. My thumb smoothing over his cheek, an angry purple bruise flourished beneath my touch as his concerned thoughts filled my head. "Thank you for being by my side." I whispered.

His mouth curled at the corners into a small smile, accepting my silent apology. "Where am I?" I asked once more. My head felt too heavy on my shoulders as I tried to look around, to study more of my surroundings.

"You are safe now," Jax replied, moving from the chair. "You're *home*." His smile spread wider when I shook my head. This was not the bare, neutral-toned bedroom of my childhood. "You're in the castle, Cassidy. Your *future* home."

My eyes widened suddenly as my pulse quickened, remembering the series of events that had led me to black out. "Where's Flynn? Is he okay?" I asked, panicked. "Did I...was I able to...heal him fully?"

"Ask him for yourself." He smiled, kissing my hand before getting to his feet. "I'll be back soon." His eyes flashed me a serious look. "Don't go anywhere. Please." I nodded. Even the effort of a simple task was tiresome.

The door creaked as Flynn burst into the room, rushing to my bedside. "Cass, you scared us all!" he gushed. "Don't you *ever* do that again." He warned as his arms enveloped me in his embrace. Despite the humongous effort, I drew my arms around him. Feeling his warmth soaking in his vitality.

"I'm so happy you are alive!" I told him. My chin resting on his shoulder, watching as Jax disappeared from the room without a backward glance. "What the hell happened? Trolls... here?" I pulled back from him. "Where's Logan?"

Flynn's eyes cast down to his lap. Something flickered within me. Anxiety? Fear? "Flynn, where is he?"

SIXTEEN

Logan

Cassidy's gaze was fierce while smothered in concern as she made her way through the large oak doors of the throne room.

"You should be resting." I told her silently as she approached. Her eyes swept over the congregation before me. Everyone's heads turned to look at her, watching as she approached, parting ways to create a path to reach me.

Her thoughts drifted back to the night of the Masquerade of Whispers, her first time being in this room, of Jax and myself as we enjoyed her, taking turns pleasing her. The blush on her cheeks grew deeper once she realized I was listening to her thoughts. She quickly replaced them with concern and confusion as her eyes drifted over me, noticing my arm in a cast and sling as well as a bandage wrapped around my forehead, covering the large cut from the fight with the trolls. I was grateful she was unable to see the cuts on my torso and knee.

"Why haven't you been properly healed?" she asked.

"The Elders sent all the healers in Estoria across the Kingdom," I informed her. *"These trolls have been attacking all over Xeyiera."*

"Why are The Elders here?" she asked, staring at their hooded figures. Only their bright-white orbed eyes were visible.

No one had ever seen what Elders looked like without their robes. Myths and rumors spoke about their actual appearance, considering they were centuries old. Immortal beings. Supposedly, their true forms could unhinge even the most stable mind.

Their presence sent a shiver along my spine, when all seven of them had appeared, demanding my counsel. Elder Jeremiah was the main authority and spokesperson for The Elders. Accompanied by Elder Bjorke, Elder Muar, Elder Quinn, Elder Nell, Elder Piotr and Elder Xion. All rules and stipulations were written by them, as decreed in the Rules of Conduct. People of Eyre viewed The Elders as if they were Gods to be feared and respected simultaneously.

"It is most unusual for any troll to be discovered in Eyre, let alone two starting an unprovoked attack against Prince Logan and another one in full bloodlust in the village of Cire," Elder Jeremiah spoke. His robe, like the others, was black, yet distinguished by a small embroidered J on the left chest. The only way to differentiate them was by the embroidered initials on their robe. "Our presence is due to the rarity of a troll attack. We must uncover the truth and the intentions of the future Princes regarding this matter."

"Where is Prince Jax?" Elder Bjorke piped up. "I thought he was with the future Queen, but now that she's here... where is he?" Her eyes were wide, tentatively wrapping her arms around me. I winced at the pain in my chest, though I tried not to show it.

"You must let me heal you," she whispered in my ear, her eyes doe-like as they looked up at me through her long eyelashes.

"No, you almost died trying to heal Flynn." I hushed back, my eyes firm. My fingers traced her jawline, hooking underneath her chin. I lifted it slightly, planting a delicate kiss on her lips, unable to hide my relief at the return of color to her face. I was grateful that the troll hadn't killed me.

"Flynn was so close to dying," she whimpered. "I owe him so much, if it wasn't for him... you'd be dead too." Her voice wavered, biting her bottom lip. "I could not let him die... just like I cannot sit by and watch your pain. I am a healer; it is what I do."

A small, defeated smile broke across my face as I planted a kiss on her forehead. "Fine, but only when you are back to full strength," I whispered. "And not a moment sooner." My lips lingered against her skin, inhaling a scent I thought I would never smell again.

"Aside from the trolls, we have also come to discuss another matter... *Cassidy*." Elder Jeremiah added, his eyes focused on her. His words were followed by a chorus of an agreement from the other Elders.

"What about Cassidy?" I snapped, instinctively using my body to shield her from them.

"We cannot allow her one month to decide." Elder Nell piped up, his voice sounding almost excited.

"Agreed. It is too long... too much is at stake, the kingdom is too unstable after these troll attacks." Elder Xion added.

"It is such a big decision, and she was already allowed this time." I told them, feeling her body stiffen beside me.

I heard her worried thoughts echo in her mind. "She's getting her thrills from both brothers." Elder Muar sneered. "Playing one brother against the other."

"I bet she loves the attention too," added Elder Piotr.

Elder Quinn, who had remained silent throughout, now stepped forward to speak, but I shut him down with my growl. "You will talk of the future Queen with respect!"

The room fell silent.

Elder Quinn nodded. "Logan, I have seen a war..." He muttered. "Blood against blood... brother against brother...."

I shook my head. It would not come to that. I tried to soothe her frantic thoughts, but we both knew I could not.

Elder Jeremiah stepped forward, raising his hand to silence the other Elders. His white beady eyes focused only on her. "Cassidy has until the end of this week to make her choice." As he spoke, the air seemed to grow cold around us, his breath visible as small puffs of smoke. "Only one brother can become King, and this kingdom needs one sooner rather than later." His voice softened. "Cassidy, there is something you need to know."

SEVENTEEN

Cassidy

I stood in silence before them, consumed by fear and confusion. My brows furrowed as I focused on Elder Jeremiah "They are both my soulmates."

"Oh, the naivety of youth she brings!" Elder Xion sneered once more.

"Yes, Cassidy, but it's a little more *complex* than that," Jeremiah said, his gloved hand reaching for mine. "It appears you do not know the full extent of this bond between the three of you."

I felt my heart start pounding against my chest.

"It's known to very few as *scissa amor vinculum*, the broken love bond." Elder Jeremiah said, focusing on me.

The Elders whispered among themselves, their raspy voices sounding like the rustling of dry fall leaves. Elder Jeremiah clapped his hands which instantly silenced them.

"Unlike the typical soulmate bond, a person has to choose to accept their soulmate by consummation. You, Cassidy, have two suitors to choose from, though it is not as simple as accepting one of them through sexual intercourse. Should you be *intimate* with one of them, it will not sever the tie with the other... It will, however, make your connection with that prince stronger than what it already is. "

"So, when Cassidy chooses, how will the bond be broken with the prince she did not choose?" Logan asked.

Elder Jeremiah was silent for a moment, his white eyes fixed on me. "Only death of the unchosen suitor will break the bond."

The room erupted into whispers once more, as my pulse raced and my head spun. *"One of us has to die?"* Logan's thoughts stirred as he shifted uncomfortably.

"How many is she bound to?" Elder Bjorke shouted over the whispers. "Is that friend of hers, Flynn, one of them too?"

I held my breath; dread gripping my heart, squeezing the air from my lungs until I could no longer breathe. *Is that why I can communicate with him telepathically? But no, surely not if his soulmate is Jace.*

All eyes were on me. An eerie silence smothered them all. In those few moments, the recollection of The Elder's abilities flooded back to me. The Elders read all minds. I cursed under my breath; *I have just exposed Flynn's secret.*

"No!" Elder Jeremiah raised his hand as sounds of Elders Nell and Xion scurried to the door. His forceful tone stopped them dead in their tracks. "Flynn is...*different*. He is not another one of Cassidy's suitors, he has this ability, because... I gave it to him." Elder Jeremiah paused; his hooded head bowed. "Flynn is my son."

The chime of the grandfather clock startled me, forcing a small yelp of shock to escape my lips. I had become accustomed to its insistent ticking as the small black hand worked its way around the clock's face, marking every minute that passed. I heard the soft whir of the pendulum as it swung underneath.

After Elder Jeremiah's revelation, his confession of such magnitude I could not fully comprehend, the Elders had disbanded. It was a cardinal sin for an Elder to interact with humans, let alone conceive a child. It all made sense now. There were small things I never understood about Flynn, like how he could manifest objects out of thin air, move things without touching them and seek lost items easily.

The Elders were renowned for their ability to read minds and detect lies, except among themselves, it seemed.

Logan had stayed behind with Elder Jeremiah and Elder Bjorke, who also confessed he had a child, and Elder Quinn, who seemed indifferent to the revelation. "I have to discuss this issue with the trolls..." He looked reluctant to let me out of his sight, his fingers tightly intertwined with mine. "I won't be long, I promise."

Each tick of the grandfather clock was a glaring reminder of how little time I had left to decide. *Who would I choose, Logan or Jax?* I could not bring myself to think of the aftermath of my choice, that one of them would be dead.

Elder Jeremiah's words repeatedly echoed in my mind. This explanation of the bond I shared with Logan and Jax was daunting and exhilarating. I found myself focusing on the same thing both Princes latched onto; *sex.*

"Does that mean...?" Jax asked, casually leaning on the doorframe, his eyebrow raised. "We can...?"

Logan cleared his throat, startling Jax, as he stood behind him, "Today is *my* day," he said, brushing past his brother, his gait staggering as he entered the room.

"Let me heal you." I begged, rushing to him, my palms outstretched. He shook his head, too stubborn to show he was in pain, though I could see it in his eyes. "Please." I pleaded with him silently, my eyes fixed on him. "You're still badly hurt."

Jax scowled, crossing his arms over his chest. His eyes narrowed as he watched Logan's arm snake around my back, pulling me into his chest while his head nuzzled into my hair.

Jax's voice pierced the silence, exasperated. "Are we just going to ignore the fact that one of us has to die?"

Horrified by his words, I buried my face into Logan's chest. Silent tears rolled down my cheeks. "I-I don't want to choose t-that..." I sniffed. "N-never..."

"Shh," Logan soothed, his mouth kissing the top of my head, burying his face in my hair.

Jax roared in anger. His jealousy overwhelmed him, his fury and hatred encircling us all. "You have no choice, Cassidy. You heard Elder Quinn. Unless you want there to be a war?"

Furiously I shook my head. "No, I don't want that either."

"It will happen," he huffed. "Whether you want it or not." Without another word, he abruptly stormed out of the room.

Time paused as silence enveloped us. Suddenly Logan winced, and his knee gave way. I grabbed hold of his shirt, tearing it open, exposing his muscular chest, bound with bloodied bandages. I stared at him, my eyes narrowing at the other cuts and grazes across his abdomen and chest. "Sit," I commanded.

When he tried to protest, I held up my hand, playfully pushing him onto the bed. "Since you are injured and in pain, you will be of no use to me today." I winked at him, "unless you let me heal you." I said, placing my palms on his bare chest, the light of my healing powers sinking into his chest.

He let out a low growl as it filtered through his skin, soaring to his injured arm. I held my breath, feeling his pain slowly ebb away as he wiggled his fingers that poked out beneath the cast. He gritted his teeth as the light moved, toward his knee. He gasped as his injuries repaired themselves from the inside out.

"You'll still feel tender but-" His lips were on mine, canceling out my words. He tore at his cast, freeing his arm so he could thread both hands in my hair. He was kissing me in an urgent, desperate kind of way while his hands moved from my hair down my body, pulling me on top of him. He held my hips as he pressed his erection against my heat.

A small squeal escaped me, as I rubbed myself against him, feeling his mouth inches away from my ear, his breath hot against it when he whispered, "I want all of you, Cassidy."

A tingling sensation pricked at his words, my longing to feel him inside. "You heard the Elders." I moaned as he began unbuttoning my blouse hastily, revealing my braless breasts. "The bond is not affected by..."

Logan let out a moan as he took a nipple into his mouth. "Only if you want it." He purred as his tongue moved onto the other breast, his tongue rolling around my nipple in tantalizing circles.

My breathing quickened, and I moaned loudly as his mouth consumed as much breast as he could. My hands ran through his hair, pulling his face away so that I could kiss him. I wanted him. Right here. Right now.

"How much do you want me?" I asked, grinding myself against his solid member, as I carefully removed his shirt. Logan tugged at his bandages now that his wounds had fully healed. I smiled and my eyes lit up at the sight of his sexy, muscular chest.

He panted as he wriggled out of his jeans. "You know I have wanted you since the first time I met you." His breath was ragged as he slid my legs out of my clothes in one smooth motion.

I felt his breath hot and heavy on my slit, and as he removed my underwear, his tongue explored my slit, tasing my nectar and making my whole body tremble.

Logan crawled over me, his tongue trailing along my body until he reached my mouth and his tip rubbed against my entrance. "Are you sure?" He gasped. "We don't have to... it's okay if you change your mind."

EIGHTEEN

Logan

Cassidy's nails dug into the flesh of my hips as she pulled me closer. I exhaled deeply as her walls stretched to accept my member as I eased it into her inch by inch.

I was enveloped by her warmth as her body yielded to me, crying out as my rock-solid shaft filled her. Her moans were melodic, driving me wild. My pulse raced as I pushed deeper, now almost fully inside her. I could feel my load was ready to burst, but I refrained. *Slow and steady*, I told myself, sliding the last few inches into her.

Her eyes flew open, biting her lip as she felt my bare skin against her entrance. She cried out in pleasure as thrusted into her.

I smirked. *"I'm shocked you can handle it... you're so tight."* I told her silently, as she arched her back and ground her hips into mine. Our lips crashed against each other as I thrust in and out of her, feeling her walls tightly grip my manhood.

She was close. I increased my rhythm, feeling her writhe to match. Her moans grew louder, and her nails pierced my flesh as she clung to me, quivering uncontrollably.

"Logan!"

My shaft twitched as her body buckled with the force of her climax. *"Tell me, is it better than the fake one you took?"* my mind asked her, turned on by the recollection of seeing her slit filled with the phallic object.

She nodded, unable to speak, her body squirming with pleasure. I licked my lips as I watched its force ravage her.

Feeling her nectar trickle down my balls, I wanted to keep making her come, over and over, until she could not handle it.

"Do you want more?" I asked silently, kissing her passionately as I drove deeper into her slick hole.

The base of my shaft brushed against her sensitive clit, and she shuddered while her eyes lit up with excitement. "Yes!" she exclaimed. Her legs automatically wrapped around my hips which I took as an invitation to bury my shaft deeper into her.

A growl resonated from my chest as I pushed on; harder and faster than before. The bedsprings groaned as the wooden bed rattled and crashed against the wall.

"E-Everyone...w-will...will h-hear us..." She panted, her voice husky.

"They already know." I smirked, gently pulling at her bottom lip with my teeth. Her face blushed, yet she continued to dig her nails in, wiggling her hips beneath mine, enjoying my shaft filling her completely.

Even though my load swelled, I held back. Jax and I had an unspoken agreement., We could both have her body, her slit. Neither of us wanted to plant a seed inside that would grow to be a child, the next heir to the throne, until she had made her choice.

She was on the brink of another climax. It felt surreal, being deep inside her, knowing that the bond that connected us would only grow stronger. Her pleasure was my pleasure which made it difficult to control my release.

Her body convulsed as if I had flicked a switch inside of her. I pulled out as large jets shot forcefully from my tip, spraying her naked torso and her perky breasts. I smiled seeing them covered in the warm, sticky mess.

Collapsing beside her, my breaths slowed from my forceful eruption. Our lips found each other once more. "That... was amazing," she gasped.

I nodded in agreement, feeling her thrum of satisfaction, but doubt niggled in my mind. I asked her silently, *"This is not enough for you to choose me, is it?"*

Jealous thoughts swirled in my head. Our bond wasn't what she had wanted. Actually, she never desired an attachment to anyone. There was nothing we could do to make her choice easier. My jealousy toward Jax overwhelmed me. *Why could it not be that simple? She wanted me; she got me. Why does she want him? Can't she ignore him as though he doesn't exist? Why can't she just choose me?*

She tensed, a hurt look in her eyes as she glared at me. It burned a hole in my chest, knowing I had upset her. *Shit.*

She rolled off the bed quicker than I could stop her. "Cassidy..."

She snatched up her clothes before disappearing behind the door to the ensuite bathroom.

"Cass. I'm sorry..." I called through the door. She was angry, and I could sense her betrayal at my flippancy with her bond with Jax. "I know it's not that easy..."

"Leave me alone," she urged, as the sound of water filling the bathtub rang out, smothering her words. "Logan, please. I-I just-need time."

I thumped my fist against the side of my leg as I spun on my heel. *Fuck.* I ran my hands through my hair, sighing in frustration.

Water trickled from the tap behind the locked door. "Cassidy, I am sorry." The thick wooden door muffled my words. "I'm scared to lose you...to *Jax*... because...I love you."

NINETEEN

Flynn

I was asleep, until the sounds of Cassidy and Logan in the room next door woke me. I was not sure if they knew how loud they were, though if I could hear them, so could Jax.

At first, I tried to block them out, but when the bed started knocking against the wall it was too hard to ignore. Instead, I found myself imagining Jace, wondering how it would feel to sink my shaft deep into his rectum, feeling him envelope my manhood with his tightness, finally accepting the soulmate bond we shared.

My hand wrapped around my throbbing member, stroking, and teasing it as memories of Jace's lips glided along my shaft, his tongue exploring every inch. I pretended my hand was his as I tightened my grip and thrashed harder, imagining his eager mouth waiting for my seed.

With an ear-splitting crash, the door hit the wall as the Elders flocked into the room. Startled to see two Elders standing before me, I tried to clear my head of the memory.

"Flynn, you are under arrest." Elder Xion's face screwed up in disgust as he ripped the quilt from over my naked body.

My manhood was still clutched in my palm. I let go quickly, as their hands dragged my naked body onto the floor. I screwed up into a ball, the cold stone floor against my bare skin made me shiver as I tried to cover myself my exposed flesh.

"Get up!" Elder Nell barked. "Get dressed." He tossed clothes from the floor onto my bed. I was in shock. *What the fuck happened? Why am I being arrested?*

"Do you know who your father is, boy?" Elder Piotr asked. I shook my head. I had my suspicions, but I could never find the proof I needed to be sure. My eyes swept across the hooded figures that stood in the room. There were only three of them. *Where are the others?* I scanned the room again.

Last night, I stayed in a guest room in the castle so that I could recover from the troll attack. I had saved Prince Logan's life. *Am I being arrested for relieving myself in a royal bedroom?* I shoved on my clothes.

"No, fool." Elder Xion quipped, reading my thoughts. "Considering your esteemed lineage, as Elder Jeremiah's son, I expected you to possess more intelligence."

I turned to face him, disbelieving what he had just said. "Elder Jeremiah... He's my f-father?" I asked, watching as the material of his hood creased as he nodded. "Is that why I am being arrested?"

"Partly," Elder Piotr replied, a dangerous grin on his face. "But mostly because of who you *desire*." He spat.

I had no time to wonder what was going to happen, as his fists rained down on my body. I crashed to my knees. Blow after blow was delivered with precision, winding me, breaking my nose, and cracking my ribs. Elder Xion was known for his violence, especially for his intolerance for gay relations. I wondered if it was because Elder Xion secretly harbored a secret, a passion not dissimilar to mine, that his violence tried to mask.

"You are a vile little piece of scum!" Elder Xion snarled, his cloaked foot connected to my stomach.

I tried to curl into a tight ball to protect myself. The searing pain rippled throughout my body. I tried to reach out to Cassidy, not knowing if she could hear me, not knowing if she was too busy to help.

"Cassidy... get to Jace. They know. The Elders... they are going to kill us!" His foot connected with my head; pain seared through my skull as a white-hot fire engulfed it. *"Please Cass... Get to him before they do!"*

Twenty

Cassidy

I did not know where I was going, but I had no time to waste. My feet smacked on the marble floors of the castle as I ran, matching the tempo of my thumping heart. *"Where is Jace?"* I asked frantically. *"And where are you, Flynn?"*

"Cass, don't worry about me, just find Jace. He's at his home. If they get there first, they will kill him!" Flynn's voice was frantic.

I felt his pain, the injuries they were inflicting on his freshly healed body. My rage fueled my feet to run faster. *"They'll kill you, too!"* I shouted back in my mind as I dashed down the staircase, frantically searching for an exit.

When I finally stumbled upon one, I yanked at it. *Fuck, it's locked!*

"Here," Jax said, appearing from nowhere, dashing over with a key. "I'm coming with you." He shot a look at me before I could protest. "Elder Maur may be alone, but he is dangerous."

I nodded, accepting defeat. He grabbed ahold of my hand, leading me outside. *"Logan, please find Flynn."* I said telepathically, before shutting him out, shame washing over me. Today was meant to be his day, and I could feel him seething about Jax's presence.

"Why isn't Logan with you? Wasn't he very good at *it*?" Jax chuckled.

"Shut up, Jax." I snapped. "Why must everything be one big joke to you?"

Jax fell silent as he unlocked the door, holding it open. I was focusing on the directions Flynn tried to issue, but the images he flooded in my mind were jumbled. I latched on to a familiar place; a fork in a road at the heart of Fic. I ran as fast as my legs could carry me, heading for that landmark, hoping to make sense of the other images once I got there.

Jax kept up my pace seamlessly, not a hair out of place or the slightest hint that he was tiring. Yet beads of sweat clung to my forehead, my muscles were tiring, and my pace was gradually slackening.

"This way." Jax motioned, taking a left turn at the crossroads. I eyed him suspiciously. "I'm good at puzzles." He smirked; his hand still clasped in mine.

We ran for ten more minutes until Jax pulled me into a narrow alley, which opened onto the street that Flynn had shown me. All that was left was finding the correct house. Jax pointed as he sprinted toward it, and I instantly recognized the white wooden door with four small glass panels.

Jax smashed one of the panels with his fist, using it to unlock the door from the inside. I winced as his wrist came away covered in blood. "It's nothing, just a scratch." Jax murmured as we stormed our way into the house.

It appeared empty, neat, and tidy as if no one was home. "He's not here!" I gasped, frantically looking around for any signs of a struggle, but Jax was already upstairs. I followed him, climbing the stairs, calling out Jace's name. That was when I smelled it, that tangy, metallic scent of blood. My heart froze. Jax and I were confronted with a ghastly sight.

Elder Maul stood over Jace's curled up body, his black robe dripping with liquid crimson. He froze when he saw us, but his white eyes narrowed. "Shield your mind." Jax rang out, as he lunged for the Elder, ripping a piece of robe in their struggle, allowing Elder Maul the chance to escape.

I rushed to Jace's unconscious body; his face pummeled into a pulp; his body broken as if every bone was smashed. I felt for a pulse, sighing in relief when it faintly beat beneath my fingertips. As I tried to summon all of my strength, flashbacks of Flynn's beating popped into my mind. *I do not have the strength to heal them both.*

My eyes filled with tears as my healing ability did not channel through my palms. Scrunching up my face to summon every last thread, I thought, *this is all my fault.* My shoulders shook as my sobs coursed through my body.

"Cass...he's breathing. Please, stop. I'll make sure other healers are available." Jax pleaded. "Jace will be safe at the castle under the Royal Guard's protection."

He planted a firm kiss on my lips, his hands cupping my face. "Don't be so hard on yourself Cass, you haven't mastered your ability yet. It drains you too quickly. Already in less than twenty-four hours you have healed more wounds than some healers have in a week." He tucked a loose strand of hair out of my face. His eyes locked onto mine. "I promise Jace will be healed, but not by you... you need to rest."

Back in the bedroom at the castle, tiredness washed over me. My muscles were exhausted and my energy was depleted, but my mind would not succumb to sleep. I tossed and turned to get comfortable, trying to shake the images of Jace and Flynn in the guest bedroom, both unconscious, being fussed over by three other healers.

"Cass, it took three healers to fix the damage The Elders had caused," Jax whispered. Hearing the creak of the hinges, my eyes darted to my door to find him trying to shut it quietly. His bare feet padded softly on the stone floor as he made his way over to the bed.

"I didn't think you would be able to sleep," he whispered, as he crawled under the covers, wrapping his arm around my waist. His scent soothed me as I took a few deep breaths, feeling the familiar guilt sweep across me.

"Cass..." He coaxed my body to turn to face him. "Don't be upset with yourself, these things are beyond your control."

Sniffing, I locked eyes with him, desperate to flood my mind with happier memories; Jax was only too eager to oblige. Filling my head with the sunset we witnessed in Verancas as we kissed on the beach, the tide slowly crashing against our feet. Those moments of passion, of togetherness with Jax, made my skin tingle.

"Would you like to see the sunrise?" he asked, his mouth brushing against mine. "We could leave now for Zeiynte's sand dunes or Trikara's hilly forest."

My eyes twinkled. *"Isn't that breaking curfew?"* I asked him silently, as my mouth kissed him back.

"Rules are there to be broken," he replied. "So, where would you like to go?"

My mind raced, seeing three people being injured in such a short space of time. I was not sure if I ever wanted to leave the confines of the safety of the castle walls ever again. *At least not while the trolls are still out there.*

"I promise you will be safe with me." Jax said, his breath hot against my skin, making me tingle all over. "The Elders have stepped in with the troll situation, well, the remaining ones. They are working with Logan... making a deal with their leader to ensure Xeyiera is safe from their attacks once more. I promise you; it is all under control."

My eyes snapped open. I had not heard anything in Logan's thoughts about this. "Cass... I have no desire to put you in harm's way; I just want to help fulfill your dreams."

I sighed, the longing to feel free beyond Eyre overcame me once more, trusting him with my safety knowing he would not do anything reckless that would put either of us in the path of danger.

"Okay, surprise me," I whispered, pressing my body against his, my leg wrapping over him, feeling the bulge between his legs press against my core. He groaned against my lips, his hips automatically thrusting into me.

"You are not making it easy to want to leave," he murmured. His words danced over my lips as he rolled on top of me. Pinning my wrists firmly to the bed under his palms, his member throbbed as he tried to bury it in my shielded heat. A moan escaped his lips. His hot breath flooded my neck. "But if you want to make it to see the sun rise..." He retreated from the bed, adjusting his manhood inside his boxers as he got to his feet. "Be ready in five minutes."

I exhaled; my core still tingling from his closeness. *We shall resume this later,* he added mentally as he dashed back to his room. I flew to my feet as adrenaline pumped through my body. *I have nothing clean to wear!* I thought. *"Jax... do you have a t-shirt or something I can borrow?"* Within moments he returned to my room, a stack of clothes in his hands.

"Being a Prince, I rarely get the luxury to wear these," he mused, handing over a pair of gray sweatpants and a plain black t-shirt.

I quickly removed my clothes, my back to him as I discarded my underwear, feeling his eyes watch me as I pulled his gray joggers over my naked buttocks and the t-shirt over my naked breasts. "How am I going to keep my hands off you?" he asked, standing close behind me, one hand reaching up under my t-shirt, pinching a nipple between his thumb and forefinger, while the other disappeared beneath the waistband of the sweatpants. His fingertips brushed over my smooth mound. "Especially when you aren't wearing any underwear...."

"Are you sure you want to leave?" I whispered as he nibbled on my earlobe. "We don't have to go."

TWENTY-ONE

Jax

There was no greater scene in Trikara than the one before me. Cassidy's naked body was bathed in the light of the rising sun, illuminating her flawless skin. Her ragged breaths made her chest rise and fall, and her back arch like a bridge over the long-stemmed blades of grass that caressed her skin. The view was beautiful from between her legs. Hearing her loud moans of pleasure as my mouth explored her.

I could not take my eyes off of her. I longed to absorb her completely, just like the morning sunlight, and bring her pleasure in every way imaginable. Her core quivered as she rode another wave of ecstasy.

"Jax…" her voice sang, as softly as bird songs in the distance. "Please," she begged, clutching hold on my hair, pulling my face back up to her. "I want you."

Her hands slid down my neck, digging her nails into my shoulders as my tip teased her entrance. I lowered myself inside her, feeling her resistance ebb the deeper I got. Her thrumming pulse was visible in the vein that ran along her neck, too irresistible not to kiss, to feel the beat beneath my lips. I had envisioned that I would go slow, be soft and sensual, but as soon as my shaft was fully encompassed in her warmth, my carnal desires unleashed.

I drove into her hard, pounding against her with all of my strength. Pinning her down with one hand on her throat, she writhed and bucked against me as she enjoyed this rough encounter. Cassidy knew what she wanted, our tryst in Alyiah's hut had opened her eyes and filled her head with dark fantasies and desires.

She wanted to be treated with love and respect, but right now, she had succumbed to her primal urges, wanting nothing but to cum over and over again.

Her hands ran along my spine, and her nails scraped against my flesh making me lose control of all thoughts, other than sinking my member so deep into her that she screamed my name.

I was not finished with her yet. I rolled onto my back, pulling her with me, shoving my fingers into her panting mouth, willing her to lick and suck them as if it was my cock, while she rode me as fast and as she could manage. Her moans caught in her throat as she choked on my fingers, her breasts slamming against her body as she slid up and down on my shaft.

I wrapped her hair into my fist, pulling at it, forcing her head down to mine, my lips crushing hers with an unadulterated passion that burned inside me. She quickly pulled away, biting on her lip to stifle her scream.

"I want to hear you," I told her silently. *"There is no one around to hear us."* She did as she was told, as the wave of pleasure flooded her body, her pants and moans were delightful, a pitch-perfect rendition of my new favorite song.

Then, my world-shattering orgasm forced its way through my body, originating in my loins. I pulled out of her just in time. Since I had not brought anything with us to clean up what was about to shoot out of me, she guided my rock-hard member into her wet mouth. Her lips clamped around it, sucking my shaft as my load exploded. Watching her swallow, it was something so indescribably hot, so unspeakably sexy, that I held her face in position until every drop of my come had been released.

I felt her tense beneath me, her eyes flickering open. Something obstructed the sunlight. We were amidst a colossal shadow. Bringing her here was a mistake...

Demi had lied to me.

Spread across the grassy terrain, spanning several feet on either side of us, was a large, imposing shadow. Seeing the outline of its large bulk, broad shoulders attached to thick, bulging arms. Hunched over slightly so its boulder-like fists grazed the long grass, walking on legs that resembled tree trunks. I knew what it was before I even looked over my shoulder to see it strolling on one of the hills.

It's a troll.

Scrambling to my feet, stark naked, I spun to face it. Despite being unarmed, I shielded Cassidy with my body. I wished I had my sword, but we were alone without weapons. I had been under the belief that Logan and the Elders had resolved the issue; that there was no need for alarm. *At least that was what Demi had said. Shit.*

I threw a look at Cassidy, who sat upright, completely motionless, her eyes wide in shock as the troll approached us. Amusement flickered in the creature's eyes as he bared his hideous teeth.

Her trembling hand slipped into mine as she got to her feet. "Run to Sophora. I will distract him." She shook her head, her fingers interlocking with mine in an act of defiance. One that, as a royal Prince, I should not take lightly.

"It *wasn't* a request, Cassidy," I told her through gritted teeth. She stiffened beside me as my guilt flooded every fiber in my body. I would not let her know my fear. Flynn was not here to help take down this troll. No one inhabited this part of Trikara. The hills were too steep to build on meaning the nearest village was several miles from here.

"I am staying with you." She bit her bottom lip, trying to stop me from seeing it quiver in her worry. "If I leave, I won't be able to heal you..." Tears flooded her eyes, unable to take them off the creature that was edging closer by the minute.

"One of us is going to die, Cass," I snapped. "At least if I die here, it will make your decision easier."

"No!" she screamed as I let go of her hand, taking a few steps away from her, giving her an opportunity to run.

"Go Cassidy. Get back to Eyre."

"I don't want to leave without you." She tried to clutch my hand, but I had already moved out of her reach. "Jax, let's go. Both of us. Sophora can outrun the troll!"

I had considered it, but it would become a hunt, a game for the troll, following us back to Eyre, destroying everything in its path. "No. Get back to Eyre. You'll be safe there. I have alerted Logan to send the guard. I will try to hold off this troll as long as possible." I glanced away from her briefly, trying to ignore Logan's furious onslaught of expletives and thoughts over my stupidity for bringing Cassidy here, for putting her life in danger. The sound of her sobs drew my eyes back to look at her once more.

Her eyes flashed up at mine as tears rolled down her cheek. *"Please don't make me do this."* She pleaded silently. *"Please don't make me leave you here."* I turned to face her, though not turning my back on the troll fully.

"You have no choice, Cassidy. One way or another, you will have to choose who lives and who dies. I'm just making that choice easier for you."

I had upset her, albeit reluctantly. The harsh sting of my words had pushed her away. I was encouraging her into Logan's arms, because at this moment of time her safety was my main priority. "Cass, go!"

Her footsteps scarpered toward the horse, before the distinctive neigh of Sophora, and her hooves thundered off into the distance. I heard Cassidy's sobs as they faded. I did not want her to worry, nor did I need her emotions to distract me. To ensure my survival, I needed to maintain focus. The guards were going to come, though it was unclear how long it would take. We had gone off the track, away from civilization. These lands were not well known. Until they arrived, I was on my own.

My gaze met the troll's as it stood just a few feet in front of me. Their sheer size was intimidating, let alone the smell. Rotten carcasses, mold, piss, and shit, assaulted my nostrils as its odor drifted toward me in the breeze. "Puny human Prince" It spat, hunching over to take a proper look at my face. "I was told I would find you here. I am Vruut, leader of my kind."

I gulped, hoping Cassidy was out of earshot by now. I took a deep breath before I spoke. "Who did you strike a deal with Vruut?"

He smirked, crouching down to my level, his repugnant stench making my stomach church. "Your sister, she promised our freedom when you become King." His eyes narrowed. "But this is more than just our freedom now, your brother killed my sons, Keib and Raab..."

Twenty-Two

Cassidy

The trees rushed by me in a blur of greens and browns. My tears stung as if being pricked with hundreds of hot needles. I tugged on Sophora's reigns, commanding her to stop at the sounds of distant voices ahead.

That was when I saw them, two heads of trolls just above the tree line, their deep voices rumbling in the air, too low to make out exactly what they were saying, but I was not going to stick around to find out. I skulked back into the shadows, as quietly and slowly not to alert them of my presence.

I need to take another way back to Estoria.

The forest grew thick and dense; the sunlight struggled to filter in through the canopy of leaves, but the mossy and damp ground muffled the sound of Sophora's hooves. I tried to remember the map in my head, inside Father's blacksmith shop. *If I can get to the river then run through the woods, I should be able to follow it north, taking me directly to Estoria, to safety.*

Sophora trampled tentatively, her ears pricked upward as we both listened for trolls or any other wild beast that might see us as prey. Wolves lurked in these woods, particularly on the quietest of nights, howling up to the moon, but all was silent. The smell of damp moss, fungi and mud grew thicker, but as we pressed forward the trees began to thin and a sound of trickling water could be heard. Tired and thirsty, Sophora galloped toward the sound.

The river was wide and fast flowing. Sophora looked for a calmer spot farther along the bank to have a drink.

"I'm sorry girl." I sighed. I looked up, seeing the turrets of the castle above the trees. *"We are so close Sophora, one last stretch, and you can rest."*

I smiled when the horse huffed and came to a stop. *"Okay, and I will also make sure you get a special treat."* Her head dipped once more into the water, before her slow strides broke into gallops. I patted her neck and uttered encouraging words to her as the walls of Estoria began to draw near.

Estoria's gates stood open, but guards patrolled the walls. Logan had increased the level of security around the city following the recent attack. They were patrolling the streets by the dozens.

It had been too dark to notice, as we left the city this morning. Yet in the light of the morning sun, a clear divide was visible. The people of Estoria were displaying who their loyalties lay with between Logan and Jax, reminiscent of the tension between my parents, neither of them agreeing on who I should choose, but on a much larger scale.

Signs were posted in front of houses, and propaganda for either side stared blatantly from shop windows. *Where had all of this come from?*

"Meet me by the lake in an hour." Logan's voice demanded. *"I will explain later."*

I decided to visit my Father, knowing he would be at his blacksmith's workshop, unable to bear the multitude of questions my mother was sure to ask. As I got closer, the furnace was so hot that it burned my nostrils, and the woodsy and molten metallic smell from the fire made me wish I had not entered the town. All kinds of weapons were churned out in assembly-line fashion. Swords, spears, daggers, arrows and throwing knives lay in various stages of completion before me.

"Papa?" I called, stepping inside, after tethering Sophora to the post. "Papa, are you here?"

"Cassidy?" he spluttered, dashing out from the shadows. His face and overalls were black with soot, and his brow beaded in sweat. As he approached, he dabbed at his face with a rag from his pocket. "What brings you here, my girl?" he asked, embracing me in his muscular arms.

"I was just passing...Papa, what is all this?" I asked, my arm gesturing to the surplus weaponry that lay on the tables before us.

"Preparations for war." He was solemn, his eyes could not meet mine as he pulled away from the hug.

"Against the trolls?" I asked, confused.

He shook his head, removing his gloves that bore dark, angry scorch marks. "*Your* war," his mouth was pulled into a grim line. "That is what the locals are calling it - Cassidy's War..."

My mouth fell open in horror, gaping at his serious expression. Father was not one to jest, especially about such events. "Sweetheart, most Estorians don't believe you will make a choice. You hold the Fate of the Kingdom of Eyre in your hands. Many are doubting your ability to decide the best-fitted Prince to be King." He slumped, as if carrying the weight of the world on his shoulders.

"Brawls have already begun in taverns, and clashes in the street have kept the guards busy. It's only a matter of time. The rumors are about your bond and that one Prince must die... the folks of Eyre are divided." He dabbed at his brow again, mopping up the fresh beads of sweat that had oozed from his pores.

I blinked as his words washed over me. "Logan and Jax... do they know? About all of this, I mean?"

He nodded, slowly, deliberately. I did not believe that Logan and Jax wanted a war. They wanted me to choose. I still had three days, including the rest of today.

"Papa... I don't want it to come to a war." I murmured, burying my face in his chest, my arms tightly wrapping around him as if I was a small, scared child.

"Sweetheart, I don't think anyone can stop it. Even if you make a choice, the people of Eyre are afraid that you will make the wrong one."

My head hung low as I left Father, my shoulders sagging under the weight of his words. *Perhaps I should have just picked one at random, like a name out of a hat or drawing straws?* I rested my head against Sophora's neck, feeling the gentle beat of her heart. Staying that way until she huffed in annoyance.

"Okay, okay." I chuckled lightly as I climbed on her back, feeling proud of how confident I felt on the majestic creature. "I am going to show you my favorite place."

The lake was calm, it unnerved more than it soothed me. No breeze stirred the leaves, and not a single ripple disturbed the lake's surface. It felt like all life had stopped and all hope was lost. Time escaped us as Sophora and I stood, gazing at the lake. Lost in my thoughts and preoccupied by Father's words, a figure appeared in the reflection on the lake's surface. The whites of his eyes pierced into my soul through the lake as I watched him approach from behind.

The initial emblazoned on the lapel of his cloak identified him as Elder Quinn. I stood in silence, waiting for him to be the first to speak, abiding by The Rules of Conduct: only speak to the Elders when spoken to.

"It appears you *and* Prince Logan have found the Lake of Lost Souls," he mumbled. "A place I used to frequent often, contemplating the many challenges I faced as an Elder. As I'm sure you are aware by now, not *all* of us were in favor of *some* of the decrees outlined in the Rules of Conduct." His voice was smooth, almost melodic, compared to the gloomy bellow of Elder Jeremiah. "Cassidy, the consequences are far greater than you think, and unfortunately, time is not a luxury you have."

"I never asked for any of this. I don't want a war to happen."

"It is too late to change that…" He was silent for a few moments. "But the decision is still yours. You should not let *anyone* take that away from you."

TWENTY-THREE

Logan

I longed to be beside Cassidy at the lake; to soak in the tranquility of her presence. But over a third of the Royal Guard had abandoned their posts ready to march to the small, fortified city of Cire, being led by none other than Demi.

She had been the ringleader in this war; the one who held the biggest spoon, and the most to lose should Jax be defeated. Not only was he her twin and her confidant, it was clear she loved him more than a sister should.

As she rallied the men, I heard her distaste when she spoke about Cassidy, the envy seeping like venom into every word she spoke. "The future queen is not deserving of Prince Jax, but it is she who has captured his heart... we must fight with all that we have for Prince Jax to triumph... to be the next King!" Loud cheers erupted from the men, who clattered their sword handles against their armored chests.

As I watched her rallying their morale among the soldiers, *Elder Jeremiah is right, there was another player in this war, though I had not expected it to be her.*

I cleared my throat to get her attention, Demi instantly spun on her heel to face me. Her eyes were tiny slits. Her arms folded in front of her chest, and she stood poker straight.

"I know the truth, Demi." I seethed, watching her move away from her convened army at the front of the castle. I followed her along the path that led to a small garden where as children we had once built dens and fought pretend battles.

A memory stirred within me, as we stood in the middle of what had once been our pretend battlefield.

At that time, the summer heat was stifling, yet we still paraded in the metal armor helmets, our wooden training swords in hand. The grass was long as it grazed our knees and wild daisies and bluebells grew unhindered. This had been my mother's wild flower garden, the only part of the grounds not pruned with precise detail and perfection. We stood on opposite sides of the lawn, Jax on one side and I on the other.

Demi clutched Jax's hand, as if the battle was real, planting a kiss on his cheek that the eight-year-old Jax did not approve of, wiping it away with the back of his hand. From the moment we charged at each other, her eyes never left him, watching his every move, wide-eyed.

Being older, I had an advantage. I was taller, stronger, and I had a bit more practice wielding a sword even if it was only made of wood. Jax was feisty, irrational, and hot-headed. He stabbed blindly with his wooden sword until it connected with my stomach. It winded me, but before I crumpled fully onto the ground, I swiped at him, catching his side so he too tumbled to the ground.

We both groaned in pain, rolling in the long grass until we both started laughing uncontrollable laughter that evoked a stitch in our side. But Demi was not laughing, her face was pulled taut, her eyes glowering at me as her hands sought Jax's.

"Please enlighten me on what you *think* the truth to be, Logan?" Demi smirked, her voice snapping me back to the present.

"I know it was you who made a deal with the trolls. You spread propaganda to rile up the kingdom." I replied calmly. "And I know that you are in love with Jax."

Her eyes flew open wide, the flicker of shame and truth spread across her face before she vehemently shook her head. "What a load of bullshit!" she hissed. "You have no evidence of any of those accusations."

"I don't need proof Demi; your secret is safe with me." I sighed. "But what I don't understand is why you want this war." That was when the thought struck; Demi was far smarter and observant than what any of us had given her credit for.

If our bond is broken by one of our deaths, then the bond could also be broken if Cassidy died.

"It was *you* that sent that troll today? Jax was never in any danger, was he?"

Demi shook her head as her eyes lit up, and she licked her lips. "Jax did not know of course. He needed to believe that the danger was real, it was the only way to separate Cassidy from Jax. I wanted Jax to send Cassidy back here alone." She paused. "I had hoped one of my trolls would catch her or that I would have met her along the path."

My stomach clenched, and my blood boiled beneath my skin. Demi stepped closer to me, putting her arm on my shoulder. "I have never liked you. You are everything Jax is not, but you would have made a perceptive *and* smart King. But both of you are blind when it comes to *her*. Your bonds to her have made you both *weak*."

Her nails dug into the flesh of my shoulder, and her eyes darkened. "What I don't understand is why neither of you can see the *advantages* of Cassidy dying. You both would get to see another day and settle this feud in a different way."

The thought of Cassidy lying lifeless and cold filled me with a sorrow so deep that it clawed at my lungs and tore out my heart. "I will not let you harm her." I gasped, feeling every breath become a struggle. "Neither would Jax."

"He will not know it, until it is too late," she sneered. "I suggest you find her and enjoy her while you still can. Come tomorrow, one of you will be dead, and I am hoping for *your* sake it is Cassidy."

I had never ridden on my horse, Mylah, so fast in all of my life; but I had to get to Cassidy, I had to keep her safe. Cassidy was asleep in the long grass when I finally reached the lake, her head propped on Sophora's resting body. It had been dark for a while now, the confrontation with Demi had delayed me from getting to the lake as promised.

I looked upon her face, her eyes red and puffy, evidence that she had been crying. Though I had not felt her once she blocked our telepathic link as she disappeared to Trikara with Jax.

I recalled the way her body reacted to my touch, how surprisingly her slit had welcomed me. I refused to think about it doing the same for *Jax,* but his scent lingered on her body. It assaulted my nostrils, made my stomach churn and my anger flare.

"It's not her fault." Elder Jeremiah had reminded me earlier. *"The bond between you all is rare. She cannot control how she feels or how her body responds to both of you."* I knew Elder Jeremiah spoke truthfully. *"The time will reveal itself when Cassidy knows in her heart, who the best suitor is for her."*

I watched over her, enjoying the peace she and the mare had as they lay in the long grass, their chests rising in unison as they slept. I moved closer, sitting beside her, relishing the silence. Being here was enough. For now.

When I left the castle, the Elders had regrouped, planning to put aside their differences. Knowing they needed to be a united front for this upcoming war. The Elders needed to remain unbiased, as should both Jax and I die, the kingdom would fall under their leadership once more.

Before Demi's revelation I wanted to tell Cassidy the good news that Flynn and Jace were now fully healed, but now Demi's plan weighed heavily in my thoughts. I did not want to alarm her, but the threat to her safety was too great to shield my thoughts. *When she wakes up, she will know everything.*

My eyes traced the soft lines of her face. Lingering on her lips, remembering how good they felt to kiss, but more importantly how beautiful they were when she smiled.

"Logan?" Her voice fluttered, as her eyelids twitched. "Logan, is that you?"

"I'm here Cassidy." I whispered, pulling her into me, feeling her arms reach around my neck and her lips press against mine. Her body molded into me, her thoughts reflecting how safe she felt in my arms. I never wanted to let her go.

"Where's Jax, is he okay?"

I nodded, smoothing her sleek hair beneath my fingertips. "He is fine Cassidy. He was never in danger." Her lip trembled, as I explained Demi's plan, not divulging too many details. "I promise Cassidy, no harm will come to you."

"Why did you not tell me about this war?" She rested her head upon my shoulder.

I tensed, my heart raced, and my voice was barely a whisper. "I wanted to tell you, but I was hoping you would decide before it came to this."

"I wish it was that simple." She sighed; her eyes lingered on my face a few moments before suddenly kissing me with an urgency I had never felt before.

I tried not to think of anything other than her, setting aside the scent of sex that lingered on her skin. She got to her feet, and a seductive grin spread over her face as she pulled the t-shirt over her head, and slid down her sweatpants until she was completely naked.

She walked to the water's edge, her hands reaching for me, beckoning me to join her as she waded into the water up to her waist. Goosebumps rose on her skin, but she did not seem to notice, fixated on one thing: *me.*

Without hesitation, I joined her. Never had I undressed so quickly, my urgency to feel her naked flesh against mine. Our lips joined moments before her legs wrapped around my waist, her heat pressed against my shaft. "Better?" she whispered; her eyes glinted as the sun faded.

"Almost," I replied.

Holding her firmly, plunging us deeper into the water, allowing it to wash over us, my hands ran along her body, removing any trace of *him*. When she reemerged from the water, flicking her hair out of her face, the scent of her skin and the faint lavender smell in her hair tickled my nostrils. *Now she smells so fucking delicious.*

Holding her buttocks, I slowly lowered her onto my length, feeling the familiar tightness grip me once more. Her legs wrapped around me to support her weight as she gyrated her hips against mine, forcing my shaft deeper inside.

"Logan," she gasped, using her thighs to slide herself up and down on my member. Her nails dug into my spine, dragging them along my flesh as she increased her rhythm. I drove hard against her as my mouth crashed against hers with the full force of a starved man, devouring her lips, holding her, burying myself deep inside. Her cries of pleasure drowned my labored breathing as the thrashing of our bodies disturbed the once still water. I was so close, but she had ignored the warning signs, too busy bucking against me, riding me to her own sweet orgasm. The peacefulness of the lake was shattered by her cries of my name as her orgasm neared.

There had never been a more perfect time than the moment of our climax reaching its peak together. Her eyes widened at the realization that it may have been too late. Launching herself off me without a second to spare, my load exploded from my shaft. *That was too close.*

I would have stayed at the lake for hours; just the two of us. The tranquil setting of our sacred place allowed us to forget everything. Goosebumps spread across Cassidy's skin but she too looked intent to stay here.

"We should go back to the castle." I whispered, not waiting to disturb the serenity of the moment as we both rested our heads against one another looking across the lake. Cassidy shivered once more, her eyes catching mine, before reluctantly nodding her head.

I draped my jacket over her shoulders as we walked beside our tired mares, our hands intertwined on one side and reins clasped in the other. The gentle clopping sound of their horseshoes against the flagstone streets echoed in the evening air.

As we approached the gates of the castle, one of the guards came rushing toward us. "Prince, the Elders are waiting for you."

The war room was aptly named for the large maps decorating the walls, depicting the World of Xeyiera and its many kingdoms. A large-scale model of Eyre spread across the central table. Miniature villages were finely detailed, but the biggest and most delicately crafted of them all was the city of Estonia. Within its large fortified walls, each brick was delicately carved and counted to make a replica of the real thing. In addition, the boroughs were precisely marked. Everything was correctly mapped, from the houses and factories to the exact number of trees. Father was a stickler for precision, especially where the safety of his beloved city was concerned.

I had not noticed the missing place initially - I had not known of the lake's existence then. It irked me, but also gave me an idea. There was a way for Cassidy to remain away from the battle, knowing that every map that ever existed of Eyre also failed to include the lake's location.

I shielded my mind from Jax, refusing to give Jax any details that Demi could extract and use to her advantage. As a plan formed in my mind, my guards advised me of what the best strategy would be; though there was an elephant in the room no one wanted to address: the trolls.

I could feel Cassidy, the lament for what was to come, her fear and heartbreak. She did not want to choose, and I understood it was not a simple choice. Jax and I had only made it worse, selfishly trying to convince her one way or the other.

Elder Jeremiah's voice echoed in my mind, *"Cassidy knows already, but she is too scared to admit it."*

TWENTY-FOUR

The moment I laid eyes on Flynn and Jace as they held hands and sat on the edge of the bed, my tears fell. Neither one of them looked as though they had been beaten within inches of their lives. Their interlocked hands rested on their laps, no longer living in fear of their love. Both of them thankful that they were alive and well, able to enjoy the peace that granted them once they stopped fearing others' opinions of their relationship.

I wanted what they had: contentment, love, and *certainty*. Knowing they would wake up beside the person they loved with their whole heart. I envied their singular soulmate bond which made it easy for them to decide; yes or no, whereas my decision was not as simple.

Flynn's arms wrapped around me, closely followed by Jace, both of them holding me while I shook with sobs. My heart was breaking and my head was spinning, envisioning my life without either Logan or Jax in it.

When I finally ran out of tears, Flynn looked at me, "You need to listen to your head Cassidy and decide realistically who is best for *you*."

"What about the kingdom?" I sniffed, dabbing at my sore and tender eyes.

"Fuck the kingdom... This is *your* life. You need someone who will *always* put you first, who will always be honest and truthful to you and who will do whatever he can to make you happy, no matter what."

Jace cleared his throat, he had been silent for the most part of the conversation. "Cassidy, your choice is the person you think about before you go to sleep and the one you think about as soon as you wake up."

That evening, as I lay on my bed, I thought about Jace's words, willing for sleep to overcome me. My mind drifted into nothingness, and all of my thoughts faded away, but with the looming war, it was not easy.

The darkness crept upon me when there was a knock on the door. My eyes flew open and I shuffled to it, still wearing only Jax's t-shirt. *Who do I want it to be?* I asked myself. *Who would I want to spend this night with?* I sighed, *Both of them.*

The thought of the Masquerade of Whispers came to my mind, recalling the thrill of having them both pleasuring me at the same time, longing for them, imagining spending the night with them both, knowing that if the war ensued tomorrow, one of them would not come back.

Someone knocked once more, and as I opened it my eyes popped out, and my jaw dropped. The two princes stood side by side with their heart stopping smiles.

Twenty-Five

"*What the-* What's going on?" Cassidy's eyes flitted between us, before they dropped lower. Her cheeks flushed a deep crimson, trying to erase the fantasy that lingered in her mind. *This is just a dream.* I heard Cassidy's thoughts whirl; *I must be dreaming... this can't be real.*

I chuckled as I stepped forward, tilting her chin up to mine. "This is not a dream, Cassidy." She looked at me with a confused, shy grin. Logan hovered over my shoulder; his aura abuzz with jealousy. Reluctantly I moved past her, taking a seat on her bed, feeling its softness embrace me, wishing we were alone to enjoy it.

Logan's eyes glowered at me, before his arms slid around her waist and drew Cassidy's body closer to his. I could feel their connection, the spark between them, and it awakened the jealous creature that lurked inside me, ripping, and tearing its way to the surface.

"Cassidy... we *both* want to spend time with you." I piped up, catching her attention as she broke away from Logan's deep kiss. A deep crimson washed over her face, and her gaze dropped to the floor.

"*This is... weird,*" her mental voice said, as she tentatively walked over to the bed.

"We know how hard this is for you, so we are both here, for you. *At your command.*" I smirked, patting the bed for her to sit beside me. I studied her, wearing only my t-shirt exposing her bare, slender legs. *I wonder if she is wearing underwear.*

Cassidy's eyebrow raised, her blush deepening, and as she sat beside me, the hem of the t-shirt rose, revealing her bare thighs. *"I suppose you'll have to keep guessing."* Her flirtatious remark popped into my mind.

Logan's eyes narrowed, watching our silent exchange as he quietly closed the door. His feet made soft padding footsteps as he approached us. His eyes were locked onto Cassidy, and like a magnet hers snapped up to him.

"Cassidy, tonight is about what *you* want..." I whispered, as my hand reached for hers, our fingers slotting together as if they were pieces of a puzzle. Her eyes opened wide, and her jaw dropped.

"But... I-I haven't-"

Logan's kiss swallowed the rest of her words.

"We're not here to make you choose between us. We are here because we are what you truly want; both of us," Logan said silently, his tongue curling against hers as their kiss deepened. *"As Jax said, we are here for whatever you want from us."*

Cassidy pulled away, looking between Logan and I, her eyebrows raised in confusion. "And you're both... okay with this?"

With a clenched jaw Logan nodded, as did I. "Obviously, I would rather have you all to myself," I purred, nuzzling her earlobe knowing my hot breath aroused her.

"As would I." Logan interjected, dropping to his knees, his hands spreading her thighs.

My heart raced as my hand slid down to her core, *I have to know how wet she is for me.* My fingers tingled as they discovered the smooth mound between her thighs.

Cassidy's sharp intake of breath made me want to explore more, but Logan swatted my hand, replacing it with his mouth. She squealed, her hand gripping my thigh as Logan's tongue mimicked his earlier motion and curled against her slit.

My jealous beast was raring to be unleashed. It was hot watching pleasure ripple through her body, feeling the same sensations she did through our bond, but it was hard to ignore the fact that *Logan* was the cause of it. *If it was Alyiah I would have no problem enjoying this.*

That's when her fingers walked along my thigh and settled over my bulge. Her gaze was uncertain. I crushed my lips against hers as I wriggled out of my pants, my hand clutched in her hair. *"I want to feel these lips elsewhere."* I purred, my fingers pulling the t-shirt over her head, watching her breasts bounce before slowly guiding her head lower onto my rigid shaft.

She licked her lips, her eyes widening, her breathing in shallow gasps as Logan increased his frivolous tongue against her clit. My shaft throbbed the moment her mouth engulfed it, feeling the soft wet warmth smother its entire length. *Fuck.*

The scene before me was hot, as I tried to imagine Logan as anyone else other than my brother. He was the only person who was trying to steal her away from me permanently.

I laid back on the bed, imagining it was just the two of us, allowing the sensation of her teasing tongue to take me to the edge of a powerful release. I felt my load swelling in my balls as the tip brushed the back of her throat, but I wanted to savor tonight. She released my shaft, gasping for breath and screamed in her orgasm as it quaked her body.

Taking my opportunity, I clutched at her hair and brought her mouth to mine, smothering her gasps with my kisses.

Cassidy

What is happening? What am I doing?

My thoughts swirled in my mind as I laid beside Jax, kissing him with unbridled passion as Logan's head was buried deep between my thighs. Every flick of his tongue sent a shiver like an electrical current coursing through my body.

This is so surreal!

Flashes of the Masquerade Ball sparked through my mind, and my pulse quickened, realizing that it was their intention to recreate that *for me.* My heart swelled knowing they had put aside their feud for me.

Logan's mouth slowly retreated from my slit, planting kisses on my body leaving a trail of my glistening nectar in their wake. The pair causally switched positions,

Logan at my side and Jax between my legs, but he wasn't kneeling; instead, he pulled my body closer to his, as his tip slowly glided over my entrance.

My whole body quivered, my wish to have them both had come true, *if only for tonight.*

Logan's kiss deepened, his back to Jax as if ignoring that his shaft was now thrusting deep inside my soaking core. My cries were stifled by Logan's lips as he pinched and rolled my nipples between his fingers.

The sounds of the slippery wetness of my slit mingled with soft pants that rose from my throat as Jax's fingers dug into my thighs. He thrust deep and hard, making my buttocks smack against him like loud claps of thunder, and my moans filled the air.

"Is this what you wanted?" Logan whispered, his words dancing across my lips.

I nodded, grabbing his hair, and crushing his lips against mine once more as my orgasm ripped through my body. Every muscle tensed and my moans came thick and fast. My core was still throbbing even after Jax had relinquished his hold deep inside my entrance.

I scrambled to my knees, my mouth wrapping around Jax's shaft, my core was for Logan's pleasure *as well as my own.*

The moment Logan drove his rock-solid shaft deep into my warmth I was almost taken over the edge, my hand working Jax's shaft, as my mouth wrapped around the tip, Jax groaned as it jerked against my wandering tongue, his breath quick and shallow.

"I'm so close," Jax said through our telepathic link. *"I don't want to cum just yet."*

I nodded, as he took each breast in his mouth, nipping and suckling at them until I could not contain my screams of pleasure.

Blush crept over my cheeks; embarrassment swallowed me whole. *The entire castle can hear us!*

I suddenly felt a pressure against my rectum, as Logan's thumb pressed against the tight hole, working it in up to the knuckle.

"Turn around." Jax demanded,

"It is my turn," Logan simmered silently.

"It still is, but trust me... Cass you will enjoy this." He scooped me up off the bed, holding me tight against him as his lips sought mine, his teeth biting the tender flesh of my neck. I bristled in annoyance. *"Why? What for?"* My thoughts whimpered in reluctance, as my body craved for Logan who was laying in a different position on the bed. Seeing Logan's muscular body stretched before me, his solid member waiting for me, wanting me, made my core tingle.

"You are going to sit on his face, whilst I make your ass mine." Jax's thoughts fluttered into my mind. I was filled with a bubbling excitement, like a shaken soda bottle ready to explode.

I bit my lip, as Jax's strong muscular arms turned me around mid-air before lowering me to Logan's greedy mouth. My clit was so sensitive I came straight away as Logan's tongue lapped at it, but the fizzing anticipation grew inside me.

Will it hurt? I wondered.

Jax's hand pushed me forward, coaxing my ass to be held high in the air, while Logan's tongue worked at the tight entrance. I whimpered, feeling so vulnerable, my fists balling into the bedding as both prince's licked and entered each hole with their experienced tongues.

Logan

Cassidy's sweet and tangy nectar flooded my mouth as she came, her screams muffling into a pillow. I did not stop, wanting to taste her, to make her cum over and over, as if that was the most important matter on my mind.

I would have made tonight a slow and passionate affair, but this was what Cassidy wanted. Jax and I both heard her lustful fantasy as she recalled the Masquerade Ball as we made our way to her room. Her urgency had us excited, and now seeing and hearing her enjoyment was enough to bring me to climax.

I wriggled my way up the bed, my shaft brushing her sensitive clit before I sunk it deep inside her. "Ride me how you want, Cass," I groaned, my hands gripping her buttocks, moving her body along my shaft, while Jax's tip teased her tight anus.

The sound of him spitting on her, made me angry, *how dare he be so degrading.* But Cassidy never cared, too lost in the moment to notice. The moment his shaft penetrated her ass, stretching it, making her slit even tighter, I felt her convulse. Cries of ecstasy involuntarily left her mouth.

"Jax... Logan..." she whimpered, her nails clawing across my chest, leaving deep scarlet lines running parallel along my torso.

"Am I hurting you?" Jax asked, temporarily stopping his actions, but she shook her head. Her lips crashed against mine as she ground her hips frantically against mine, bringing herself even closer to climax. She used my shoulder to stifle her mouth, which angered Jax.

"I want to hear you scream my name!" Jax demanded, his fingers tightening around her throat. *"You are going to come so fucking hard. You will never forget it."* He promised.

Cassidy rode my shaft, her warm hole soft and yielding as I thrust my hips. *Fuck, why must I share her?*

My nails left small crescent marks in the peachiness of her ass, as I drove against her movements, until she was rendered breathless. Sweat trickled down my brow, and beads of sweat glistened all over her body.

Jax's eyes caught mine, our agreement reinforced silently. *Neither of us were to cum inside her,* but both of us were close to teetering the dangerous line. Jax's mouth pulled into a taut line.

"But... her ass... there is no risk there." Jax tried to reason using the telepathic link.

Cassidy's eyes lit up, delirious with desire, as she frantically nodded her head. *"Yes..."* She panted. *"Do it. Fill my ass with your load."*

"Fuck... Jax" Cassidy gasped as her tightness enveloped me. Her pleasure rippled through us both as every hole was filled. *I am so fucking close.*

Logan took her nipple in his mouth, nipping at each of them as she thrashed against us, biting her lip to stifle her screams.

"I want to hear you..." I growled, forcing her mouth open with my fingers as my other hand wrapped around her throat.

Logan shot me a warning look, *"Cut it out Jax,"* he said silently, yet I continued, ignoring him.

I could no longer control my possessiveness of her body, my jealousy reared inside me like a serpent, strangling every inch of remorse I may have otherwise felt for this assault on her body. *Her ass is mine, and she will cum over and over, whilst he monopolizes her slit.*

"You like it rough, like this, don't you Cass?" I asked, chuckling when she tried to nod her head, feeling her walls hold me in a vice-like grip. Logan was seething, but he could not deny her slippery thighs and the nectar that coated his balls as we both sank deeper into her warmth.

Sweat was trickling along my spine, her body tensed as my shaft throbbed uncontrollably once more, feeling her nectar cascade out of her like a gushing river, saturating the bedding beneath us. *Fuck.*

My hand tightening around her neck with each spray of my load into her tight asshole, hearing the squelching, slippery sound when I slowly withdrew. I watched the thick white globules of my seed trickling down her body and coating Logan's cock.

Fuck that was good.

"Cassidy, fuck-" Logan roared as his member thrust deep in her, his fingers dug into her ass cheeks, holding her in place. I watched as he used my cum as lube, fucking her harder and faster until she screamed out his name before her body quaked with her final orgasm.

I expected to see him move quickly, to pull out as his muscles convulsed, seeing him lose control as he came. But even as I dragged Cassidy off of him, I knew it was too late. A rivulet of his cum trickled from her slit and down her inner thigh. She was breathless and in shock.

We all were.

"Cassidy… I'm-" Logan whimpered, his eyes full of apologies, his mind a whirl of regret and remorse. He knew what he had done, he had crossed the line; broke the mutual agreement we had made.

Cassidy shook her head, too stunned to speak, her body spasming and rocking in the aftermath of her climax. "Logan… it's… okay… it felt…" Breathless and exhausted, she collapsed on the floor by my feet. *It was just an accident,* she thought.

But I knew better; I knew he had lost control. Mr. Perfect was unable to contain his lust and had broken his own promise. *What good was a king if he could not keep his word? What if she became pregnant with his child, but chose me?*

My mouth pulled into a taut line, staring at her as she scrabbled off the bed, away from both of us, looking frightened like a deer caught in headlights. I caught her eye, her thoughts spinning about the consequences, as we all were. *What if she becomes pregnant… with his baby?*

I was blinded by fury. Logan had tainted her, trying to breed with her before she had made her decision. "Are you trying to force her to choose you?" I hissed, dragging him off the bed, landing a punch or two into his naked torso. *"You're a selfish prick,"* I added mentally, my eyes narrowing at him as I slammed him against the bedroom wall.

Cassidy yelped, but I barely paid her any attention. "Jax… please stop!"

Logan

"It is *not* oh-fucking-kay Cassidy," Jax growled, his eyes shooting me a look as sharp as a dagger. *Shit, that was not meant to happen.*

My chest swelled as regret suffocated me, my lungs burning as the reality sunk in. My words clogged the back of my throat, when I tried to speak my voice cracked and nothing but inaudible sounds left my lips. *I wanted to fill her with my load. I wanted her to choose me, to have a child with me.*

Jax's hands wrapped around my neck, his thumb pressing hard against my windpipe. He actually wanted to hurt me, and I feared that he might just kill me.

"Stop it!" Cassidy screamed, trying to pull Jax's arm away from me, but his focus was solely on me.

Jax's face contorted with unfiltered hatred, his mouth turning into a snarl. "Next time I see you, it will be on the battlefield. You will be the one who dies, Logan. I will not hesitate."

I was paralyzed, I knew he meant every word, and I deserved his wrath. His eyes still locked on mine as they glowered in hatred and his words dripped with venom. "Nor would I hesitate to plunge a blade through the heart of your child, should she bear one."

Suddenly he was gone, the door slamming behind him.

It was silent in the room for a few moments, Cassidy sat hunched in a ball on the bed, naked and sobbing silently. I padded over to her; each tentative step filled my head with more doubts. *Why did I do that? Why couldn't I stop?*

"It's all my fault." Cassidy sobbed. "I should have moved... Logan..."

"Cass, it is not your fault." I soothed, my arms wrapping the duvet around her naked body, as goosebumps pricked her skin and her teeth chattered with the icy chill that had flooded the room after Jax's exit.

I sat beside her; the silence palpable. "Logan, would he... would he actually *do that- if... if I was?*"

I wanted to ease her worry, but I could not bring myself to lie to her. Instead, I pressed my forehead against hers, sharing with her a memory from my childhood

It had been my tenth birthday, all I had wanted was a pet, so when I opened my eyes and a small ball of ginger and white fluff appeared wearing a red bow, I was ecstatic. My life revolved around it, brushing off sword practice and even playing "battle" with Jax. He became furious, threatening to drown the thing if it ever left my sight. A few days later our father demanded my attendance and refused the cat into the Map room, so I had no choice but to leave her behind. When I returned, she was nowhere to be found, her red bow untangled and left on my pillow. I searched high and low, eventually seeking solace in the depths of my mother's wildlife garden, heading for the hidden tire swing I had made the previous summer. There she was, my beautiful beloved kitten, hanging limp and lifeless in the rope.

I felt her shudder as she pulled away quickly, fresh tears filled her eyes. "Will you... will you stay here with me tonight?" she asked in a whisper. "I don't want to be alone."

Twenty-Six

Cassidy

Logan's confession scared me, making me realize I knew very little about either of them. They were still strangers, but there was something about being in Logan's presence that made me feel like nothing or no one could harm me.

"Why don't you have a bath? I'll get the bedding changed." Logan smiled apologetically, his eye contact was evasive, his thoughts shrouded by regret and remorse.

I nodded, keeping silent. I disappeared into the bathroom, allowing the hot steam to fill my lungs, trying to forget about how disastrously my fantasy had ended.

Once in the tub, water lapped over my body. Every part of it pulsed in the aftermath of ecstasy, but the euphoria and thrill of living my fantasy was short-lived. My thoughts were foggy and confused. I still felt the sensation of Logan's seed as it shot into my slit. Filling it with his load was forbidden. The brothers had agreed that it was taboo until I had chosen, but Logan had lost control. *I had lost control.* Logan's warm trickle of seed dribbled down my inner thigh as I backed away from them both. Shock sucked the breath from my lungs, and made my blood run cold. *It had been too late. Fate will decide my future now.*

I submerged my face, washing away their scent, wanting to erase it all. But I could not forget the feel of them, as they both took me, stretching both entrances, feeling filled to the point of explosion as they both drove deep inside me. The orgasms were mind-blowing. My selfishness yearned to have each of them in every way. *Why couldn't we have stayed that way, the three of us? What prevented them from ruling together?*

Tradition? Their pride? Why couldn't every night be like this; the three of us, coming in unison?

My sobs took me by surprise. The impending war shattered any fantasies of what could have been. Tomorrow, one of them will be dead. The only survivor shall win my heart and body. The bond that bound the three of us together would be broken. My mind conjured images of their battle, tightening my chest like a vice. Images of both dying made my stomach churn. *Which person should wear the crown?* I asked myself as I sank back into the water. *Whom can I envision not being part of my life?*

The night was long and restless. Vivid nightmares disturbed my sleep. Silent tears spilled down my face. When I woke up, I needed to escape the castle quickly - to escape from it all. I glanced across at the sleeping Logan, my heart swelled.

The lake seemed to be calling to me, as if I was a lost soul it was beckoning to join their deep waters.

"Cassidy, why are you still awake?" Flynn's voice cut through my thoughts. *"and where the fuck are you going?"* he asked, his voice tinged with worry when I didn't answer him. *"Cass, let me come with you."* He sounded as though he was in pain.

"No, Flynn. You need to stay there in the castle!" I told him firmly. *"You are an Elder's son... the less you know, the less they can blame you for not stopping me."*

"Who are you talking about; the Elders or the Princes?" His tone sounded bitter. *"Cass, was it you that convinced the Elders to abolish Clause 4a?"*

Clause 4a was the biggest and most feared in the Rules of Conduct. It outlined that no one could partake in a sexual and romantic relationship with the same gender. The clause also carried a most severe punishment; execution without trial. Flynn and Jace were lucky, protected by the princes they could be free to love one another but outside of the castle walls, many people in Eyre continued to live in fear, hiding their true sexuality. If the clause was abolished, many people would benefit from it. They would be free to be happy and to love freely.

I smiled, creeping down the staircase, remembering the way to the main entrance. *"That wasn't me... Perhaps it was Elder Jeremiah? How is Jace now?"*

"He's great, we're great... Cass, if it wasn't you then I think it was Logan... Jax may have saved Jace, but that was only because of you. Logan... he is different, he acted because it was the right thing to do. Sitting beside me as the healers flitted around, talking to the Elders for hours. He seems to have more of an impact, he is respected by them, especially my Father..." He was silent for a moment. *"You should know something..."* He stayed quiet for a while. When I lifted the latch on the door, I discovered it was locked. I cursed silently,

"What is it Flynn?" I asked impatiently, as I spun on my heel. *What direction did Jax take me earlier this morning?* Curiously, I disappeared down a small corridor. It seemed familiar. *I think this will lead me to the-*

"Demi was behind the troll attacks... she planned it... Logan was supposed to d-"

"Die?"

"They didn't know I would be there. It was a fluke that I was. I overheard the Elders talking earlier when they thought I was still unconscious. The trolls may have some involvement in this war...seeking revenge for the trolls that Logan and I killed."

The smell of cooked food wafted in the air; the roast meats and boiled vegetables from the dinner I did not eat. I regretted it now as my stomach growled. *I am heading in the right direction.*

"Shit! Flynn... Does Logan know?" His silence was deafening. *"Flynn, warn him. Please. I-I just can't stand by while they kill each other. I don't want to have any part of this... I love them both."*

This morning, we walked through kitchens and a small door at the very end which had led to another courtyard, beyond that was the stables. Familiarity swept over me as I recognized the scenery while retracing these steps, finally reaching the stables.

Sophora was awake, and surprisingly she did not seem alarmed when I stepped into her stable, and as I began to fasten her saddle. It was as if she knew I was not meant to be here, keeping her sighs and huffs of annoyance to a minimum, but that I needed to get away. In less than fifteen minutes, I rode silently on her back through the secret and unguarded back gate, taking the same exit Jax and I used earlier.

"Cass, whatever you are doing... wherever you are going... just be safe. Okay?"

Twenty-Seven

Logan

Ear-splitting sirens rang out, jolting me out of my slumber. Hurried footsteps flooded into the room, surrounding my bed in an instant. "Prince Logan, it is almost time." Esan bowed.

Esan, my right-hand man, my most trusted warrior and counselor, had been absent after his wife had given birth to their second child. I wanted to enjoy his return; he had been sorely missed. But as I took in the scene before me, it made me want to hug Cassidy at least one more time.

Already in suits of armor, Esan and ten members of my royal guard stood before me, each carrying pieces of my armor, and several weapons. My heart raced. I had been trained to deal with war, or the threat of war, but nothing could prepare me for the adrenaline that coursed through my veins, or for the fear that filled my heart.

"Where... is Cassidy?" I asked, my eyes flitting around her empty room, while they tried to dress me, fixing the metal buckles. Esan looked at me, his eyes serious, cold.

"She's gone."

I quickly turned to see who spoke. It was not one of my guards. Leaning against the door, in a pair of black jeans and a white t-shirt, his floppy hair was now back to its usual color of wet sand, and his blue eyes were glassy, his expression worried.

"Flynn?" I scowled at him. "Where did she go?"

He shrugged.

His flippant attitude riled me, angered me. "Flynn, I swear if anything happens to her...."

"Cass couldn't be a part of this. She loves two people who are about to kill each other." His voice was soft, but I was not in an understanding mood.

I grabbed the scruff of his collar, my temper flaring as I stared into his eyes. "Where the fuck is she Flynn?"

"I don't know, my Prince," he said calmly. "What I *do* know is this war won't be fair."

I released him, recalling her face, trying to reach out to her. She hadn't blocked her thoughts; I could feel her presence in Eyre. *The Lake! I need to get to the lake!*

I shoved Flynn aside, not giving him another thought, and pushed through the remaining guards. I ran as fast as my legs would carry me; half dressed in my suit of armor. It was bulky, uncomfortable, and as hot as the fiery pits of Hell itself. Esan's footsteps thundered behind me, even the loyal lapdog followed like a little lost puppy. He was a fierce and skilled fighter, though he looked slight and scrawny. His agility was far superior and his stamina was almost on a par with mine.

"Prince Logan!" he shouted, hot on my heels. "I must insist that you stop! We must go prepare the men!"

"I have to get to her."

Halfway down the dusty deserted street, near her father's shop, Flynn's voice pierced my mind, and I screeched to a halt.

"Jax is using the trolls in the war. The Elders believe he will win should he succeed in getting their full loyalty. Logan, Cass needs you to win. She may not know it yet, but I have known her for her whole life. You are what she needs. I will not forget what you did for me, for Jace, for people like us. I just hope for the sake of Eyre that you win."

Cassidy was exactly where I thought she would be: sitting at the lake's edge. Her head rested against Sophora's body. Her tears glistened on her cheeks in the early sun's light. I approached her, knowing that she could hear me.

Flinching, she spun around until she was facing me, a small dagger grasped in her shaking hand. "Cassidy..." My eyes cast over her. "What-"

"I'm not- no. It's for protection," she sighed, lowering her hand.

"Do you even know how to use it?" I asked, my concern spread across my face and my heart hammered in my chest. She shook her head, lowering her gaze to the floor and letting the dagger fall from her hands.

"Logan... I can't do this. I don't want to stand idly by while the two of you..." A single tear rolled down her cheek. "You need to know. Jax-"

My body propelled itself to embrace her, a hand cupping her cheek. My voice was barely a whisper. "I know about the trolls." Her eyebrows raised. "Cass, I-" Gazing into her eyes, I could feel myself falling for her all over again. My thumbs brushed delicately over the rosy skin of her cheeks.

"Cassidy, I love you." I blurted, my eyes never leaving hers. "You are the first thing I think of when I wake up, the last thing I think about before I sleep, and every moment in between. I would do anything for you. If you asked me to, I would crawl through fiery pits of Hell, climb Mount Hejha, I would even give up the throne. All I want, all I need, is you."

Brimming with tears, her eyes glazed over. She blinked forcefully, refusing to let them fall. "Logan..." she hushed; her breath flitted across my lips. I savored her closeness.

"Cassidy, I want you to understand that my feelings for you go beyond this connection. It's more than just lust. We are more than just being Fated to be together. You are my world."

Her lips fluttered against mine, her arms wrapping around my neck, pulling my body closer to her. "I-I love you to Logan. but..." She didn't need to finish the sentence. I picked up the dagger from the floor. Her eyes opened in horror. "What... what are you d-doing?"

"Just in case it's best that you know how to use this," I told her, putting the blade in her hand, clasping my hands around hers on its handle. "Keep your grip firm, tuck your thumb around it like this. When you thrust, move with your full body, use your body weight to give you momentum."

Together, we moved forward, stabbing the air before us. I let go of her, watching her continue the motion. *"Do not trust anyone, especially Demi,"* I added silently.

My heart was beating hard. Her hand was trembling, the tip of the dagger scratching against the armor. She tried to smile. Sobs escaped her as she clung to me. "I can't lose you," she whimpered. Her kisses grew desperate, while tears rolled down her cheeks.

"Jax cannot be King..." Her eyes still locked onto mine, our foreheads pressed against one another, "but I cannot condemn him to death either."

I stared at her, my head and my heart filled with hope. Our kiss was disrupted by the shrill call of the siren once more. In my arms, as I inhaled her scent, I knew I had to come back to her. *No matter what.* Even though the thought of killing my brother churned my stomach, not as much not coming back to the soft embrace of Cassidy's arms.

"Stay here, away from the battle," I told her, my lips lightly brushing against hers. Adrenaline and hope coursed through my body. "Promise me, you will wait here."

Twenty-Eight

The sirens startled me, though I had not been sleeping. Jace, Cassidy and the impending war consumed my mind, preventing fatigue.

A multitude of events unfolded in the past few days, surpassing anything I had ever experienced. My near-death experience, and the looming threat of war had made me fearless, had given me the strength to disregard the consequences and seize opportunities. Last night was the happiest moment of my life. I had been able to love openly and freely without the scrutiny of watchful eyes, without the fear of punishment for not loving the correct person in the correct way. There were no words to describe the sacred act of consummating our bond. Only that it was fucking fantastic.

We laid beside one another, talking, creating plans for a future. With the absolution of Clause 4a, we were allowed to be together. We had freedom to love without punishment. Driven by excitement for the future, and desire that swelled within me, things escalated rather quickly.

Only in moments when I knew I was truly alone would I allow myself to fantasize about taking him, strengthening our bond through intercourse. We were Fated; it was natural, only sordid, and secretive because the Elders had made it so.

It felt perfect. In the castle's safety, protected by the knowledge that someone had convinced the Elders to erase Clause 4a, *I had to have him. There and then.*

"Would we stay in Fic?" he asked, his head propped on the pillow as he turned to face me. "Or would you want to leave Eyre completely?" I gazed at him as time stretched on. His skin was no longer mottled with bruises, his blond hair was soft and not matted with blood, and he no longer winced in pain.

"I don't care where we are, as long as I am with you," I told him, tracing his face with my fingertips.

His lips crashed against mine, hunger burned in his eyes, lust seeped from every pore as he rolled on top of me, crushing his shaft against mine, his muscular torso naked and smooth. His tongue was frantic in its search to entangle with mine. "Flynn," he murmured, "I need you."

I shoved him onto his back, my mouth kissing every part of his body with unadulterated desire, staring at his midriff, my lips parting around his solid member. Thrusting his hips forward, his length fully entered my mouth, pulsating under my tongue, sinking deeper until it pushed against the back of my throat.

My nose pressed against his stomach, taking every inch to maximize his pleasure. Everything about this moment felt right, how it should have been all along, not the sordid and rushed moments we had stolen before now. His hand ran through my hair, clutching a small tuft of it between his fingertips slowly crushing my face further into his abdomen as his member reached further down my throat than it ever had before.

His guttural moans vibrated through his body, tingling beneath my lips. The desire to please him motivated me to continue. My mouth tightly suctioned around him, moving my head along his length in a steady rhythm, hearing his moans grow louder. I felt it jerk and twitch as his muscles shook moments before his cum shot down the back of my throat.

Instinctively, I swallowed, his hands holding my head in place whilst he bucked and writhed beneath my lips. Slowly I retracted from him, expecting him to repay the favor, when he frowned. "Turn around," he whispered. "Face the mirror."

I saw in the reflection his lips trace over my shoulders, leaving tingling sensations in the aftermath of his touch. He reached to the bedside table where a bottle of rose oil had been left. I raised my eyebrows. His smirk was sexy. I felt my shaft harden, as he poured some onto his hand, smoothing it over my buttocks, between the crease of my cheeks. His fingers worked the tight entrance. My hand instinctively rubbed my member. *This is really happening.* My member throbbed, feeling him add more oil, easing the resistance.

"Look in the mirror," he whispered, his words hot in my ear. "I want you to watch me fuck you. Witness our bond as it grows stronger before your very eyes."

I gasped as his tip slid in slowly. He added more oil as he thrust his hips toward my buttocks.

Pain shot through me as his member stretched me further than his fingers ever had. I bit my bottom lip to stifle a whimper. His hand wrapped around my waist, tugging at my shaft, feeling it turn rock hard in his grasp.

With each thrust of his hips, his shaft rubbed against my prostate, sending a shiver along my spine, gradually transforming the pain into pleasure. The pace he thrust matched the rhythm of his hand as he stroked me, my breath coming in short, quick pants.

I cried out as he drove his hips deeper. He splashed more oil onto me until his bare torso was against my butt cheeks. Our naked flesh slapped together as I pushed back against his shaft, our moans of pleasure ringing out in unison.

I struggled to watch in the mirror as the pleasure that washed through my body forced my eyes to close as my carnal groans escaped my lips. My orgasm hit me like a ton of bricks, so sudden and so forceful that it took my breath away. My body convulsed violently, my entrance gripping his throbbing member tight, milking his load as mine sprayed uncontrollably over his stilled hand.

Gasping, my legs like jelly, I collapsed on the bed. My heart beat inhumanly fast, thundering against my ribcage, as my pulsing member slowly softened. His smirk was unforgettable, his eyes wild and sexy as his lips sought mine. Soft and tender kisses as my hard and heavy breaths finally slowed. Our connection grew stronger as his thoughts were of complete satisfaction.

I opened my eyes, staring into the depths of his, my longing to feel the sensation he had. Jace's hand ran through my hair, his hands cupping my face as a smile crept across his face. "I love you Flynn." He murmured, "I could not ask for a better soulmate."

I kissed him, confessing my love to him in our new telepathic connection, feeling my need to take him igniting deep within, until my shaft was hard once more. His fist tightened around it, as I licked my lips.

"My turn."

TWENTY-NINE

Logan

The sun broke through the thick canopy of ancient trees, casting a soft amber light upon a clearing that was to be the battlefield. Flanking me on my right was my second-in-command Esan, and the rest of the royal guard on my left leading the rest of my loyal warriors standing behind us. Across the clearing was my brother, my flesh and blood, along with his band of personal guards, and his council of warriors.

In theory, my numbers compared to his, meant I should be victorious. My army significantly outnumbered his three to one. Without seeing his expression from this far afield, I sensed his stance: confident and smug. My scouts spotted his secret weapon; the trolls, a little over five miles away, along the mountainous borders of Vrek and Svaalgard. I should not have been surprised, our father had instilled many of the ancient proverbs, and *"The enemy of my enemy is my friend,"* had been one of his favorites.

I promised Cassidy I would come back for her, my confidence placed on the numbers, in my strength. I was driven by my longing to have her, forever. Despite the trolls' overwhelming presence, Flynn and I were fortunate in our battles against them.

War drums pounded in the distance with a loud and slow rhythm, each beat resonating through my bones as two lines advanced in sync with their cadence, closing the gap, inch by inch, until I could see the fierce determination chiseled into his features. Hatred and rivalry were ablaze in his eyes like two fiery beacons. The atmosphere that lay in the few meters between us crackled with tension as we both prepared for the beginning of the end.

This battle would conclude our struggle for her heart and for the throne, bringing with it the end of our brotherly bond by the death of one of us. As I gazed upon him, my inner conflict waged its own war. Mother passed away giving birth to him; *if I were to take his life now, her sacrifice would have been for nothing.*

I shook my head; I was doing this for the good of the Kingdom.

Time seemed to play out in slow motion as the two sides clashed. Swords that brandished in the hands of warriors gleamed like liquid fire in the harsh summer sunlight. There were blades dripping with blood reaching into the air. With a swift, fluid motion, we lunged at each other, our steel swords crashing like thunder. Our movements, animated like a dance, and were testament to years of strict training.

I knew his next move, as he did mine, even without using our telepathic connection; we trained and sparred together since we could both walk and talk.

Showers of sparks flew each time our swords clashed. The weight of our legacy, the burden of history, pressed heavily upon me. *What would our ancestors think of this war, this needless conflict?* My warriors clashed with their own kinfolk. *Were we dishonoring everything our forebears had accomplished?*

I envisioned Cassidy, standing alone by the lake with only the dagger and Sophora for protection. The vision of her stunning beauty was overwhelming, the urge to be near her so intense that it clouded my focus momentarily, allowing Jax to gain the upper hand. His sword arced through the air, and when it came toward me, its blade grazed my cheek, slicing the skin as effortlessly as a warm knife through butter.

As pain lanced through my cheek, and warm blood trickled from the wound, I struggled to adhere to the strict self-discipline Father had instilled in me. The foremost rule was, *"Do not act out in anger. Rash and foolish actions could be lethal."* I evaded his subsequent attack; my shield connected with his torso, briefly knocking the wind out of him.

Staggering backward, he roared in fury. *"Now."* His internal voice hissed as he straightened. Tremors rattled the land, signaling the trolls' arrival. My eyes scanned across the impending shadows; my skull rattled with the vibrations of their footsteps. There were too many to count, but the figurehead leading them was distinctive. Demi's blond hair billowed behind her as she guided the trolls to the battle.

Gasps came from warriors, and the fighting paused as their eyes fell upon the trolls. They were taller than the ancient trees that surrounded the battlefield, and the massive figures proceeded into the clearing. Teeth bared in grotesque grimaces; brandishing weapons far larger than any of my men.

I watched in utter silence as they descended, and as Demi got lost among their stampede, Jax flinched and doubled over, tears streaming down his eyes. When the dust settled, my eyes found the source of his pain; the mangled corpse of his twin and her horse lying in a pool of blood.

I expected some warriors to run from the trolls in fear and self-preservation, but I was wrong.

These beings that sided with Jax, who sought vengeance for the trolls I had slain days prior, had merely enraged my warriors. Their arrival had spurned a deep hatred for Jax, and their collective anger at putting themselves and their families in danger resulted in a sudden blood-frenzy.

With a snarl, as realization dawned upon him, Jax launched a relentless assault upon me, trying to catch me off-guard, but I was familiar with that trick. I pushed away his barrage of blows, blocking his every strike. Jax's attacks slowed as fatigue set in, and every action he took was awkward and clumsy.

I seized my chance to inflict injury upon him. My blade sliced his thigh as blood gushed like a waterfall from the wound. His deafening howl of pain pierced my eardrums, a wail of pure anguish escaped his throat, raw and animalistic as his fear of being defeated permeated his thoughts.

In retaliation, his blade sliced through the air with ease, cutting off the arm that held my shield.

THIRTY

Jax

Logan crashed to his knees, clutching at his wrist, whimpering as he stared at the space where his hand had been attached. He was now at my mercy. Seeing him fall like a broken toy to the ground. His skin was deathly pale as his life force pulsated out of his wound, draining him at rapid speed. His consciousness was failing, as my sword hovered over him. One downward thrust was all I needed to end it all; to make Cassidy mine.

His eyelids flickered, becoming too heavy to keep open as he tried to keep his gaze on me. The song of battle continued all around us, though seemingly distant and muffled as the blood pounded in my ears. As I stood over my brother, a flood of memories played out in my mind.

Flashbacks of our childhood when I used to follow him everywhere, looking up to the brother five years my senior. Logan had been my idol; who I aspired to be like. He was fearless, yet kind-hearted and fair. He had helped raise me when our father was too busy with his duty as King. Without our mother, it was Logan who used to tuck me into bed, and read me a nighttime story. He had taught me how to ride Sophora and how to communicate with her when my father had grown impatient with me.

Without Logan, where would I be? Without the love of my brother, I would have been neglected, forgotten about. Father made no secret of his loathing of me, his wish was that it had been me who had died rather than his loving wife, the Queen. Living in Logan's shadow had made me bitter. I had overlooked the sacrifices he had made. I had been too ignorant to acknowledge the acts of kindness and love he had done without a moment's hesitation for me. Even down to the succession of the throne, he had accepted our father's words without argument. He acknowledged my ability to usurp his rightful throne.

I thought of Cassidy. *What would she think if she were to see me now? If she could see the monster I had become?* I saw her standing before me, as clear as if she was truly here. Despair, horror and disgust would be etched on her face as tears rolled down her cheeks.

"Goodbye," he whispered.

I should have been overjoyed: Cassidy would be mine, along with the throne. Yet my sadness smothered me. The fire that had once blazed in the pit of my stomach was now snuffed out. My anger ebbed away, replaced by grief.

"Regrettably, brother..." I murmured, staring into his eyes. "We both know this is the only way it can end." I tightened my grip on the hilt, my palms sweaty in my nervousness and apprehension. I watched as his eyes closed for the final time. "Goodbye, Logan."

THIRTY-ONE

Cassidy

Elder Quinn's words repeated in my mind; *"The decision is still ultimately yours to make."*

As I felt their blows upon one another, I scrambled on Sophora's back, not hesitating another moment longer. The urgent pelting of her hooves against the earth echoed through the dense forest, as we headed toward the sounds of the war.

My heart beat faster, and the closer we got, the louder the battle cries were, I tried to grapple with the decision that overshadowed us all. To choose between Logan and Jax, my two bonded mates, two people that held my heart in different ways. Both would have different impacts on my life. With Logan I felt protected, loved, whereas with Jax, I felt sexy, playful, and at ease. Having traveled more with Jax than I ever had in my life, I had already unlocked that dream to be free from Estoria and Eyre. *I don't want to give up on that dream. I do not want to be trapped here like everyone else for the rest of my life.*

In the distance, the orange glow of sunlight filtered through the leafed canopy overhead. It initially seemed that there was no end to the vast forest. The air was thick with the scent of pine. Sophora pushed forward, galloping harder than before, as the tree trunks flew past in a blur of shades of brown. Absorbing its beauty, I tried making out distorted shapes that distracted me from my inner turmoil. The urgency of such a decision had inflicted a sharp pain in both temples. *I must decide;* I scolded myself, *Logan or Jax.*

Sophora stopped as we sat on an edge of the clearing, as the battle waged on before us. Bodies lay scattered, their blood staining the once green grassy field. The din of metal upon metal, swords against swords, and swords against shields rang out. The racket was enough to deafen me. Too much blood had already been spilled. *I need to put an end to this, once and for all.*

Sophora turned her head to look at me, as if checking to see if I had made up my mind. I nodded firmly, squeezing her with my thighs, pressing the stirrups against her body, urging her to advance to the battle. "Don't be scared," I whispered, though I wasn't sure if I was trying to comfort her, or myself.

As she galloped through the battlefield, the clash of steel filled the air. The metallic scent of blood lingered as a searing pain like white-hot fire consumed inside my body. So intense was the pain that I almost fell off Sophora's back. She reared up, snapping me back to attention, as I grappled onto her reins, holding on for dear life.

Time stood still as my eyes found them; the two Princes locked in a deadly stand-off, their eyes ablaze with fierce determination to prevail. But the pain still seared through me, and that was when I spotted it; Logan's severed hand among the grass. It was a gruesome yet poignant reminder of the brutality of the fight, a reflection of the unforgivable lengths Jax would go for love and power. The sight of his bloodied limb lying on the ground beside his shield made my blood run cold, sending a shiver along my spine.

My gaze shifted to Logan crumpled on the ground, clutching his right arm with Jax's sword hovering over him. *How could he do this to his own brother? If he could endure his brother's agony and be so barbaric in his actions, how would he treat me? How would he treat the Kingdom?*

At that moment, I had no time to think, only act. Hearing their words echo through my head, saying their last goodbyes, I knew if I did nothing, it would be too late. I encouraged Sophora to run straight to them, gripping the reigns tightly in one hand as I unsheathed the dagger with the other.

I had no idea what I was doing, allowing Sophora to weave between the clashes of men, narrowly avoiding getting hit ourselves, as my heart boomed in my ears. The closer we got the more urgent Sophora's hooves became.

"Jax!" I yelled out to him. "Jax, stop!" My words were lost amid the chaos, as the fighting continued around them. Sophora plundered through the thick of it, rearing up once again, unexpectedly.

Her cry alarmed me, and I felt her weaken instantly. I looked down, seeing blood cascading out of her like a waterfall. Her legs gave way and she crumpled to the floor, taking me down with her. I scrambled away from her, clutching a hand over my mouth. Nausea swept over me as she lay there lifeless, her bloody entrails exposed on the ground beneath her.

I'm sorry Sophora, I thought, as I turned my back on her. She was yet another innocent life slaughtered because of my indecision. Guilt flooded me as I staggered towards them, my vision blurred by tears.

"Jax!" I yelled, pain shooting through my side as I realized in my fall, my dagger had embedded itself into my side. Tearing it out I shrieked in agony, my hand useless to staunch the blood that oozed from the wound. It was not fatal, I would heal, it was Logan's wound that worried me more; feeling him slowly slipping from my thoughts. His presence in my mind was fading. *I love you Cass, please never forget that.*

My stomach twisted and my heart froze, Logan was saying his final goodbyes. *No!*

I ran towards him when Jax's hands stopped me by clutching at my shoulders and staring at me in disbelief. My body went rigid beneath his touch, my sight fixed on Logan, watching the color drain from his face as his butchered arm bled out.

"Jax, let me go!" I yelled, but his grip tightened, his fingers digging into the flesh as he trembled. "You're choosing *him?*" he asked, his voice barely audible as the fighting ensued around us.

I nodded, "Jax, you must go. Now." I spat. "Go and never come back." I yanked myself out of his grip, rushing down to Logan, holding his face in my shaking hands.

"Logan!" I cried, pressing my forehead to his, my tears cascading down my face. "Logan, please don't die... I-I... choose you." I felt Jax's anger, his hurt, even as the distance between us expanded as he took heed of my words. Seeing him flee the battle through his very eyes as he disappeared through the shadows of the forest.

I knew my dream to be a free bird exploring the kingdom was gone, but as I clutched at Logan, nothing else but him mattered. That was when I realized the shadows that fell over the two of us. The seven Elders surrounded us, their presence on the battlefield halted the fight.

"That was not a wise decision." Elder Quinn uttered. "One day you will regret not sinking that dagger into his neck when you had the chance."

I shook my head, *there will never be a time where I would regret saving Jax's life.* Too much blood had been spilled, too many innocent lives lost for a war that *I* could have prevented. I should have known deep down it was always going to be Logan. The stranger at the lake who had taken my heart the moment his lips had touched mine.

"You have to help him!" I screamed at them. "He is dying!"

Elder Xion scowled, "Perhaps we should let him. You made your decision by letting Jax run away."

"No!" I wailed, clutching Logan to my chest, cradling his unconscious body. "Please save him!" My gaze sought Elder Jeremiah, "Please!"

Epilogue

Cassidy

Estoria is healing. It will take a few years before it is restored to its former glory, to the strong standing it held in Xeyiera before the war.

Despite the battle scars, all boroughs are now fully operational. It had only taken Logan eight months to right most of the wrongs from the war. *My War.*

Guilt crept over me, as I thought of all those lives lost because of my indecision. It often kept me awake at night and filtered into my dreams. Though I know I was not the sole person to blame, Demi had been the mastermind encouraging the rapid escalation among the divide in the kingdom. Had she not meddled, things might have been different.

I took a deep breath, trying to clear the image of the war and instead embrace the changes Logan had implemented with his new and most trusted counselors; Elder Flynn and husband-to-be Jace. The biggest change was the Elders' latest revision of the Rules of Conduct to be inclusive to all by setting aside all past prejudices; decriminalizing same sex relationships as well as the use of phallic toys.

As I gazed down at my large silver diamond engagement and wedding rings glinting in the hazy morning sun, I wiped at a stray tear that escaped my eye. It was comforting that memories of our wedding day washed away lingering images of the war.

It had been perfect, held in the grounds of the castle on a gorgeous summer's day. The gardener had been teasing the roses for weeks so they weaved through the wooden arch that was to be our altar. It was a fixture that was made specifically for the occasion and it stood now as a permanent one on the grounds, a constant reminder of the best day of our lives.

The ceremony itself was a private affair, just our close friends; Flynn and Jace, Logan's most trusted guards as well as my family. Afterward we celebrated with the locals who threw a big party outside the castle. We even snuck off to our sacred place, the lake, to make passionate love in the place where we had first met.

Every day I woke up beside him, flooded with happiness, and the passing of time made it easier to ignore the little niggle of yearning for Jax. He was in Xeyiera somewhere, and that bond remained until one of us died. It was something Logan and I never discussed. Over the past few months, feelings I had once shared with Jax were buried beneath the love and loyalty I had for Logan. My heart had acted on the battlefield that day, and while neither of us wanted to see Jax again, it did not mean we wanted him dead.

Logan's arms tightened as soon as he felt me stir. He nuzzled my ear and whispered, "Good morning my queen." Shifting his body closer to me, his bulge pressed against my buttocks.

"Good morning my king." I murmured back, my insides melting as his face rested in the crook of my neck. His breath was hot against my skin, flitting along my neck and collarbone. They were soon replaced by soft fluttering kisses.

Logan's hand moved up to my tender breasts, gently caressing each one. I let out a moan as his fingers brushed over my nipples. They had become incredibly sensitive so only the lightest touch was enough to send a flood of pleasure through my body.

"Did the baby wake you?" Logan whispered, his hands delicately tracing circles around my hard nipples.

We had been overjoyed at the discovery, a month after the war was over, the result of that night I had shared with both Logan and Jax. A night I would *never* forget.

When his fingertips danced over my skin, they left tingly sensations in their wake, as they returned to his new favorite place on my body; the swell of my stomach. I loved how his desire never faltered as my body adapted to hold the life growing inside me, instead it seemed he lusted for me more now in the ripeness of my fertility.

Logan had a fierce loyalty, and he was determined to protect us from harm, placing us as a higher priority than that of his kingdom. *He is a great king, but an even better husband.* He always put me and our unborn child before everyone else and wanted nothing, yet gave me everything I could have ever wanted or needed.

Logan moved as I rolled onto my back, his mouth trailing my neck down to my torso. He planted a kiss just above my belly button at the same time a sharp, shooting pain shot through my abdomen. There was a swift, strong kick from the baby inside directly underneath Logan's lips.

His eyes lit up, and a smile curled on his lips. "Did you feel that?" He whispered in hushed excitement. I nodded.

"Our little Prince is going to be a powerful fighter... just like his papa," I whispered, my finger pointing to his chest. I lifted his face back to mine, and our eyes met. his chin to draw his face back up to mine. "It's a boy?" he asked, his smile growing and eyes twinkling with unconditional love.

I nodded, as a smile crept across my face. I knew that it was his dream; to have a son who would inherit the lands and the King's title one day, to strengthen our ties and keep his brother as far away as possible.

"How do you know?"

"Elder Quinn." I murmured as we broke apart. "It was one of his visions."

A cold brush of metal swept across my face as Logan's artificial hand clumsily tried to move my hair out of the way. He scowled when his limb missed its target. It pained me that I wasn't able to heal him, but I guess, I could not heal severed limbs. When he struggled the guilt squeezed my heart. Had I been at that battlefield a few minutes earlier, perhaps I could have stopped Jax's brutal attack. Yet Logan refused to let the loss of his hand sour his mood; ensuring that even with a metal limb it would never stop him from being intimate and loving.

"I'm sorry I didn't get to you sooner." I whispered; my eyes fixed on his new hand my father had made especially for him.

"Cassidy, never apologize for things that are not your fault." He smiled. "I love you, and I thank my lucky stars that I have you. I am the happiest man that ever lived, with or without the hand."

"I love you too, Logan." I fell silent. *If only I had just-*

His lips were upon mine once more, as unexpected, and as urgent as they had been when we first met by the lake. Logan's body hovered over mine, his member brushing against my naked heat. I wanted him again. I would never stop wanting him; in my arms and between my legs.

"Logan," I purred as he entered me slowly, evoking him to deeply thrust his entire length inside my warmth.

He stared into my eyes as he drove his hips against mine. "I am so glad you chose me, Cassidy," he murmured, before his lips sought mine once more.

He built up his momentum, but the closer I got to the brink of ecstasy, a dark shadow clouded my mind. An ominous feeling washed through me as my orgasm gripped my muscles and convulsed around Logan's shaft.

My breath hitched, as an unknown force clenched my soul.

This was when I felt Jax's presence, and heard his voice echo in my mind as loud as if he were laid in the bed beside me.

"One day Cassidy, you will be mine."

About The Author

Raven has been weaving narratives that traverse a myriad of genres and topics since childhood. Through her journey as a writer, Raven has honed a distinctive voice that resonates with readers, spinning tales of adventure, romance, mystery, or of fantastical realms and ethereal entities. In each intricately crafted page of her books, she embarks on journeys to places afar with lovable and relatable characters, inviting readers to escape from the reality and monotony of everyday life.

As a wife and a mother of two, life can be chaotic, yet Raven still dedicates as much of her free time as possible to bring to life ideas from her vivid imagination, in the hopes her readers find her stories transformative, inspiring and entertaining, with the aspiration to share this gift with audiences far and wide.

When she is not outside tolerating the unseasonable British weather, you will find Raven as a consistent online presence on most social media platforms, where she offers regular updates and new insights for upcoming releases. She is always happy to chat with her readers and followers.

Find Raven's other books or leave a review on Amazon or Goodreads

Website: https://www.ravenleitheharlow.co.uk/
Facebook: Raven Leithe Harlow – Author
Instagram: @ravenleitheharlow.author
Twitter/ X: @RavenLeithe

SCAN ME

Printed in Dunstable, United Kingdom